MORE MYSTERIES FROM THE
BERKLEY PUBLISHING GROUP...

A Little Traveling Music, Please

Margaret Moseley

BERKLEY PRIME CRIME, NEW YORK

This is a work of fiction. Names, characters, places, and incidents are
either the product of the author's imagination or are used fictitiously,
and any resemblance to actual persons, living or dead, business
establishments, events, or locales is entirely coincidental.

A LITTLE TRAVELING MUSIC, PLEASE

A Berkley Prime Crime Book / published by arrangement with
the author

PRINTING HISTORY
Berkley Prime Crime edition / July 2000

The Penguin Putnam Inc. World Wide Web site address is
http://www.penguinputnam.com

ISBN: 0-425-17551-0

Berkley Prime Crime Books are published
by The Berkley Publishing Group,
a division of Penguin Putnam Inc.,
375 Hudson Street, New York, New York 10014.
The name BERKLEY PRIME CRIME and the BERKLEY PRIME CRIME
design are trademarks belonging to Penguin Putnam Inc.

PRINTED IN THE UNITED STATES OF AMERICA

10 9 8 7 6 5 4 3 2 1

For my beloved niece and nephews

Robin
David
Mark
Steven
Kevin
and
John

You Mustn't Quit

When things go wrong, as they sometimes will,
When the road you're trudging seems all uphill,
When the funds are low and the debts are high
And you want to smile, but you have to sigh,
When care is pressing you down a bit,
Rest, if you must—but never quit.

Life is queer, with its twists and turns,
As everyone of us sometimes learns,
And many a failure turns about
When he might have won if he'd stuck it out;
Stick to your task, though the pace seems slow—
You may succeed with one more blow.

Success is failure turned inside out—
The silver tint of the clouds of doubt—
And you never can tell how close you are,
It may be near when it seems afar;
So stick to the fight when you're hardest hit—
It's when things seem worst that YOU MUSTN'T QUIT.

AUTHOR UNKNOWN

One

My dog got a key in Thursday's mail.

It came in a soiled white envelope with no return address and a smudged cancellation mark that looked like it came from the Balkans or maybe New Jersey. It was addressed simply to *Bailey* with my Washington Avenue address right here in Fort Worth.

The envelope was hand-delivered by my postman, who rang the bell at my door by turning the black, old-fashioned key bell. I think he just wanted to try out the bell because he *knew* Bailey lived with me—was part of my household. Sam the postman had certainly feigned enough fear when he'd delivered my daily mail as Bailey had tried to catch him in the act of lifting the mail flap in the door.

I had to call Janie Bridges—my other house-mate—to hold Bailey while I answered the ring and collected the envelope. Yes, I agreed, it was strange to have a letter delivered to a dog. The world was strange now, hadn't he noticed? And, yes, it was going to be a hot fall; the leaves prob-ably wouldn't even change until November. And thank you. And good-bye.

"For Bailey?" Janie asked about the envelope.

"Seems so. Guess I should open it though?" I joked.

"I should say so. What if it's a poisoned dog biscuit? I bet it is. And from the postman, at that." That's my Janie. Always on the lookout for the dark and dangerous side of life, she lived, breathed, and ate mysteries. Came from years of selling mystery books to customers in her con-verted gas station/bookstore in West, Texas, a long stone's throw away from Fort Worth. Now she lived with me. I liked to think it was because she had no place to go when she left her husband. However, I think it was because lately it seemed I was always stepping into mysteries and murders more often than Bailey left deposits in my back-yard.

"So open it," Janie demanded.

And so I did. The key fell out of the tear I made in the envelope. It landed with a *plonk* on the hardwood floor of the foyer. I reached for it before Bailey could scoop it up with his teeth but not before he had a good sniff at the brass object. As I closed my hand around the key, Bailey took off running in circles around Janie and me, barking to beat the band.

"Anything else in the envelope?" Janie asked.

I tore open the rest of the dirty envelope and looked on both sides of it, but the key was all there was. "Nope, nothing else." I reported. "Hush, Bailey."

Janie took the key from me and examined it. "Who would send a key to a dog? And why?"

"It's a mystery to me," I said and slapped my hand against my mouth, but the words were out there, hanging in the wind.

"A mystery? Yes, a mystery." Words cannot describe the look on Janie's face. Pure bliss would be an understatement.

I tried to take control of the situation. "Okay, okay, it's no big deal. Just a key, after all. We'll figure it out, but in case . . . just in case . . . there are any dead bodies with this mystery," and I added what I thought was a joke to the circumstances, "promise me, Janie. This time, *no* screaming."

She didn't hear me. Her eyes glazed over, and she held the shiny key up in the air like the Holy Grail. Suddenly, as I watched the bright, swinging key, I remembered the dream I had during the night, and my eyes glazed as opaquely as Janie's.

There is comfort in dreaming an old nightmare. The tall angled ceiling of the long, crooked hallway that leads inevitably to the same dark room is as familiar as the veins on the back of my hand; a hand that reaches ahead in the despair of a troubled sleep and touches air. There it is again—the rasping noise that signals the sighs and whimperings of the room. I know the sounds come from behind the desk. I remember that, as I begin the seemingly never-ending fall that culminates in a jarring crash to the floor beneath the desk. There I cower, my glasses flung far from my searching fingers. Blindly, I peer into the shadows. Blindly and thankfully. It is almost over. I just have to scream, and it will be over. I will wake up safely. Just one scream . . .

When I was a little girl, my father would rescue me from the aftermath of the nightmare, taking me by my hand and guiding me through the house as we searched for the source of the demons that had disturbed an innocent sleep. The two of us would wind up in the kitchen, eating cookies and making milk mustaches. He died when I was eighteen, but the comfort of his presence is still with me. *"It will be all right, Honey. There is nothing to be afraid of."*

I had struggled to sit up in bed. My new life form comforter is the umpteen-pound Labrador retriever named Bailey, and he stood over me on the bed, a scraggly paw on each side of my body. His black eyes were filled with concern as I said the right words to end the nightmare. "It will be all right, Bailey. There is nothing to be afraid of."

We trooped down to the kitchen, the same one my father and I had sat in years ago, and I poured Bailey's milk in a bowl after I opened the new package of Oreos. "You can't eat chocolate, sweetie. It's dog biscuits for you." We slurped and munched the last traces of the nightmare away.

I let him lick the white stuff from one of the cookies as I asked him, "Bailey, I haven't had that nightmare in ages. Don't you think it's strange that when things are going well for me—the best they've ever been, in fact—that I would have it now?" I broke apart a cookie and let him enjoy the innards of another Oreo as I pondered my own question.

"I have all the money in the world. A fantastic job. Good friends. Men who love me to the point of craziness and . . . you." Bailey took a forbidden bite of the chocolate part of the cookie and sat back. He glanced at the open package on the kitchen table and then back to me. I closed the cookies with a raised-eyebrow look at the expectant dog. "Don't press your luck, buddy."

Back in our upstairs bedroom, Bailey quickly claimed his own brightly flowered pillow, and I don't think he heard me when I asked, "I have it all. What could possibly go wrong? And another thing," I told the uninterested dog, *"I don't wear glasses. My vision is twenty-twenty. Why would I need glasses in a dream? What is it I need to see?"*

As I stood and watched Janie do her mesmerizing trick with the key and felt Bailey snuffling eagerly by my side, I realized my world was getting ready to tilt again, and I did not need this in my life.

Two

Unfortunately, Bailey's key was not all that came in the mail. Sam had also handed me several other envelopes, ones I ordinarily would not have opened. There were bills from Texas Electric and Southwestern Bell. I take these unopened to my accountant and personal financial adviser, Steven Bondesky. He pays all my bills.

Not that I couldn't. I mean it is *my* money. It just makes it easier for him to keep my expenses for income tax purposes. Lately, I have taken to just stuffing them in a large envelope and sending them on to him. I frowned at the envelopes in my hand.

Sensitive to a point, Janie asked, "Something wrong?"

I shook my head. "I don't think so, but I thought I just sent my bills to Bondesky. Can't believe I'm already getting more. Did I sleep through a month?"

Janie grimaced, "Hardly. I don't think you've been getting any sleep at all. I hear you up at all times of the night. Not that I blame you. Those last murders were awful. Just awful." And her round face clouded up as she remembered the destruction and waste of life we had just experienced over in east Texas.

In distraction from the memory, I nervously opened the electric bill.

"Janie, it says here that they are going to cut off our electricity!"

"What?"

"Yes, cutoff is today. Wait; let me look at this one from the phone company. Janie, I haven't paid my phone bill."

Janie took both bills from me and reexamined the contents. "What on earth?" she asked. "You know Mr. Bondesky has paid these. Or Evelyn. They're so efficient. You better call them and straighten it out." Then she laughed. "While we still have a phone, that is."

We were still standing in the foyer by the front door, so I just turned and went to the phone there. It's on a small table next to the shelves containing my late father's miniature horse collection, a small and sentimental reminder of the man who had loved me so. I absently patted the brass rear end of the largest horse, a replica of Man 'O War—minus a foreleg. I smiled as always as I remembered the day I had broken that leg. My finger pushed the automatic dialer for Bondesky's office phone.

"What will I do with Bailey's key?" Janie asked while I waited for someone to answer.

"Here, I'll take it," I answered and reached for the key, which I laid alongside a small jade horse on the second shelf. "Funny, there's no answer."

"Try again. Maybe they're out for lunch." And Janie headed toward the kitchen. "I'm going to make us some lunch. Tuna fish sound okay to you?"

"I've pushed it twice. Not even the answering machine. This is so strange. Yes, tuna is fine. And iced tea, please."

I continued to listen to Bondesky's phone ring. It was a lonely and eerie sound. I could imagine the ring echoing throughout Bondesky's office.

"Leftover coffee okay with you? Our water is turned off." Janie stood in the doorway with a surprised look on her face.

"The water's off? Janie, what on earth?" I repeated her earlier exclamation.

"You better go over there...to Mr. Bondesky's," she declared.

"Yes, I should. I will. But, Janie, this scares me. Why wouldn't my bills be paid? Bondesky always takes care of it."

"Maybe you ran out of money," she guessed.

"Janie, you know I have four million dollars. You helped me pack it up to take to his office, remember? All the electric, telephone, and water bills in the world don't cost four million dollars."

She put a finger on her cheek and asked, "Now tell me again. How well do you know Steven Bondesky?"

Good question, I thought as I drove from my south-side home to Bondesky's west-side office. I knew him well, I decided. From when I was a little girl. In fact, you could say I had inherited him from my father. Steven Bondesky had been my father's accountant and had made investments for him.

They had also been involved in some financial schemes involving inventions—which was what my father was—an inventor. And a kinda of patent person. I never have really understood it all, but I'm sure it was all on the up and up with my father. With Bondesky, I felt the jury was still out.

However, I did as my father had told me to do

and trusted the tough-speaking accountant to help me after father died. That was when I was eighteen, the year I graduated from Paschal High School and a day after my father died. Which was exactly a day after my mother died. You might say I was thrust into real life at a young age, but because my parents were older when they had me, I had been drilled all my life to expect just such events. I knew from kindergarten what to do when your parents died, and calling Bondesky had been at the top of the list.

At twenty-nine I can look back and see how unprepared I was to cope, but with the help of friends like schoolmate Steven Hyatt and the shrewd Steven Bondesky, I had made it this far with little damage to the body or psyche.

Well, slight damage.

I hadn't counted on all the deaths that had occurred in the past few months.

With my mother's instructions ever in my ears, I handled death pretty well. I remember crying when she told me that a cousin of a neighbor had died. She'd sniffed her inherited postnasal sniff and said, "Now, Honey, why are you crying? You didn't know Mr. Phillips. Save your tears for someone you cared about. No sense in wasting good tears."

And so I had waited and then cried over the

death of Steven Miller—the garage attendant who had appointed himself a guardian angel—and for Clover.

I had cried for Clover.

Which thought brought me back full circle as I pulled onto Steven Bondesky's asphalt parking lot.

I hadn't seen Bondesky since we both cried over Clover's death a few weeks ago.

I looked at the empty parking lot, the tall grass growing in the cracks in the walkway, and the water starved petunias in the stone containers by the entrance.

Where was Steven Bondesky?

And where was my money?

Three

In the South—and we consider Texas to be in the South—we *yoo-hoo* our arrivals, so I did the appropriate call at the front door of the office and then at each of the windows. Then I banged on all of the above, but with the same futile results. No answer. Nobody.

Or . . . no *body*.

Maybe, I thought, Bondesky was in there—in his office—dead. A few months ago, that would have been a foreign thought to me, but, hey, when you live with someone who thinks Lucrezia Borgia was a heroine and you keep falling over bodies by the score, you change your point of view.

I remembered the new prefab building Bondesky had erected in memory of his late good friend Jimmy, who I called Jimmy the Geek and whose body had been one of the ones over which I had fallen. The building was called Jimmy's Place, and the door was always open, and the coffee was always hot. Mostly derelicts and policemen dropped by and took advantage of the air-conditioning, free donuts, and clean rest rooms.

I thought, as I went around the back to the metal building, what if someone had stopped by, someone new, and had killed them all? Then had headed into Bondesky's office and did away with Bondesky and his secretary Evelyn Potter? I tend to think like that now.

I passed on the Southern hello call and just pushed open the door to the building.

Inside, it was dark and shadowy.

No one was there.

I switched on the overhead light.

The coffeepot was empty, and no donuts lay on the plate by the pot.

I was just about to turn off the lights and leave when I heard, "What the hell?"

"Who's there?" I called as I stood with one hand on the exit door.

"Who's *there*?" was the response.

"Me. Honey. Bondesky?" I asked into the area of the voice. It didn't sound like the accountant's frog voice, but I had to make sure.

"No, it's not Bondesky. Where is he?" asked the man who came out of the rest room into the light.

Seeing the man who emerged did not restore my recent lapse of faith in human nature. I kept that safety grip on the door as I said, "I don't know where he is. Who are you?" *Besides being Mr. Clean,* I said to myself.

This giant of a man, bald to a fault, came toward me with deceptive speed, reaching the door before I could exit. With his huge restraining hand on mine, he asked again. "Where is Steven Bondesky?"

I went straight to the heart of the problem. "Am I in danger here?"

He laughed and removed his hand. "Not from me, honey. I'm just trying to find Bondesky."

I sighed. "I don't know. I'm looking for him myself. I'm afraid he's dead."

"Dead?"

"Well, everyone I know lately has died. And, yes, he must be. He's never not here. Is that a double negative?"

"A double what? And who are you? His honey?"

"No, well, I'm Honey, but Honey Huckleberry. I'm one of Mr. Bondesky's clients." I backed away from the big man, out into the sunshine of the day. He followed me.

"I'm a *client,* too," he said. "And *Mr.* Bondesky owes me some dough."

"And your name being . . ."

He stared hard at me, screwing up his eyes so that they disappeared into wrinkles in his tanned face. "Sledge Hamra. I'm a PI."

His proclamation overcame my natural snicker to his name. "A pie? You're a pie? What does that mean?"

Sledge Hamra rolled his eyes, causing them to do more tricks in his face. I had never noticed before how eyes become so important in a head without hair. Of course, I had never met anyone as bald as this pie before, either.

"P-I. Private investigator."

"Oh."

"Is Honey Huckleberry your real name?"

"Is Sledge Hammer yours?"

He laughed unexpectedly, then stared at me some more. Finally he said, "Actually my name is Alvin Hamra. That's spelled H-a-m-r-a . . . not *hammer.* My friends call me Sledge."

"And they are legion, I am sure. But tell me, Mr. Hamra, where do you think Bondesky is? And Evelyn? How long have you been looking for him? I mean, how long has he been missing?" We walked toward the main building as we chatted these pleasantries.

"I've been out of town. Got in last night. I've been trying to reach Bondesky by phone for almost a week now. No answer. So I came out here. Just got here a few minutes ago. What's your story?" We stopped by the front door.

"Steven Bondesky pays all my bills for me. And they haven't been. Paid, that is. So I came out to see him. Should we call the police?"

"Nahh. We'll just go in and take a look-see. Okay with you?" He gave me a sideways glance.

"Sure, whatever you think." It occurred to me that my five-foot-two slight frame would be no match for whatever Mr. Hamra wanted to do, anyway.

"You sure have funny colored hair," he said as he whipped out a strange knife-looking object from his baggy gray slacks.

I watched as he did something with the knife and the lock. "You're a funny one to be talking about hair," I retorted. "Is that legal?"

Hamra—I didn't know him well enough to think of him as Sledge—turned the knob and opened the office door. He stopped and looked at me again. "How much money do you have invested with Bondesky?"

"A bunch," I admitted.

"Yeah? Well, so do I. Makes me think we own

part of this establishment, don't you think?"

"I buy that," I agreed, looked around to make sure no one saw us break into the office, and followed him into the building.

Four

Bondesky's office was about what you would expect a deserted building to look like. Nothing remarkable. No clues.

No dead bodies. Not even a whiff of one.

"Disappointed?" asked my partner in break-in.

I was indignant. "Of course not. What? You think I *wanted* to find Bondesky dead? I just thought we would find something that would give us an idea of where he is. He was so depressed the last time I saw him."

"Ha! So we're looking for a suicide note? If we find it, it better have instructions on how to get my money." The big man kept inching his way around the office.

Evelyn Potter's area, the reception room, was

clean and sterile. Not even the desk drawers revealed a single personal item. Only letterhead stationery and a box of tissues.

It was the old man's office that would hold the clue to his whereabouts, I thought as I went in the opposite direction of the professional investigator. Sledge Hamra headed toward Bondesky's big desk, and I went toward the little gray file cabinet in the corner.

"Tell me again how well you know Bondesky?" he asked as he began to rummage through the drawers of Bondesky's desk.

I felt behind the file cabinet for the metal box that held the key and covered my action with saying, "Oh, for years and years. I used to come here with my father when I was a little girl. Bondesky's computer was the first one I ever saw. Of course, it's changed now. Modern computer. Bondesky says Dell is the best. That's what I have. A Dell and a Dell laptop. Seems strange to see his computer turned off. I don't think I have ever seen it off before."

As I babbled, I opened the file cabinet and went straight to the file marked Huckleberry. Instead of the huge, thick file I remembered from previous visits, there was only one neon orange file with my name on it. "What kind of computer do you have?" I asked to the man across the room as I reached inside the color-screaming file.

"What are you doing over there?" He started across the room.

I palmed the object in the file and turned just as he approached. "I thought I would find something in here. This is his special client file, but my file is empty. See?"

"My name is not here."

"Maybe you're not special," I guessed.

Hamra gave me a disgusted look and continued to rifle through the files. "All this is garbage. I bet he kept the real info on the computer. See if you can get it to work." It was a demand, not a request.

I sat down behind Bondesky's desk—a first for me—and switched on the computer, which did its buzz and hum to wake up. "It's password protected," I told him.

"What does that mean? Password protected?" Hamra hovered over my shoulder to look at the screen.

"You're computer illiterate, aren't you? I should have guessed when you didn't answer about what kind of computer you had." I was sure some smugness had seeped into my voice. After all, I had owned and operated my own computer system for over two months now. I was a pro. I went into my instructor voice, *à la* Evelyn Potter, who had taught me the basics. "All PCs—that's personal computers—have the option to be secured by their owners. You can choose to input a private code word so that someone else can't access your files."

"Skip the lecture, Honey. I understand codes. So, what's Bondesky's, do you think?"

"Now, Mr. Hamra, how on earth would I know?" I could guess, but I wasn't going to share that *info* with the Jolly Green Giant.

"How much money do you have?" he asked unexpectedly.

"You're going to rob me?"

"God, of all the ditzy dames to run into . . ."

"Because if you are, I have only twelve dollars and thirty-two cents on me."

It was amazing to see Hamra run his hand over his bald head like he had a full head of hair. He said in what was obviously a very patient voice, "I asked because if you're in the same situation I am, you want to know what happened to Bondesky and what happened to your money. And if you want to know as badly as I do, you'll start trying to figure out Bondesky's security password. *Now.*" And he shouted the last word.

"Okay, okay. I'll try." And I keyed in the obvious: *Bondesky.* Then, *Steven.* Followed by

Money, Secrets, Legal, and *Illegal.* Nothing. I tried *Dell* and then the word *Password.* All were rejected by a buzzer, which sounded like a wrong answer on *Wheel of Fortune.* I even vainly put in my name, but to no avail.

"What about his date of birth?" asked Hamra.

"I don't know his date of birth," I told him.

"I'm going to look in the gray file cabinet. Maybe there's something in there about him."

While he was across the room, I typed in the word *Clover,* and the computer came to life with a tinkle of *ta-da* music.

"What was that?" Hamra wanted to know.

"It means we've overloaded the computer," I replied as my right knee pushed the glowing red button at the side of the desk. The screen groaned and went dark.

"We've killed it?"

"Yep. I wouldn't know how to get it back," I lied.

"Damn, and there's nothing here in these files that gives me a clue, either," he said.

"Well, this has been fun and all, but I've really got to run now," I told him.

Hamra put a restraining hand on my arm, "Not so fast. You're my only clue."

I've been called a lot of things—happens when

your first name is Honey—but never a clue before.
"No, I'm clueless," I retorted. "And I'm outta
here."

"How will I find you?" he asked.

"You're the pie, you figure it out." I snatched
up my purse and ran out of the building.

Five

"Where's Bailey's key?" I asked as I ran into the house.

Janie walked into the foyer. "Ask him. He hasn't left it for a minute."

And there was the blond lab, sitting patiently by the tall shelves, right where I now remembered I had put the key that came in the mail.

I was astounded. "He knows it's for him?"

"Obviously," Janie replied. "And he ate the envelope. But what did you find out at Bondesky's?"

"That he's gone, and I met the most awful man who's also looking for him. And I found this key." I held up the object I had found in the colorful file that had my name on it.

"A key? Is it the same key?"

"I'm going to find out now." I reached for the key just as the telephone rang.

I looked at the caller ID. It was my best friend Steven Hyatt in Hollywood. Ordinarily, we played a word game with unknown poets when we talked to each other on the phone. It was a habit we had started back when were both misfit teenagers and each other's only friend. Corny, I know, but an affectionate habit we still delighted in.

But not today. I was impatient as I answered the third ring, "Yes? Steven? What?"

To my surprise, he didn't react to my rudeness. "I have bad news," he said.

Well, that would explain his lapse in the game. Mine was due to the two keys I held in my hand, trying to figure out if they matched.

"Oh, no. What?" I asked as I folded the keys together in my palm.

"The movie sucks. Big time. The preview audiences hate the ending. We've canceled the opening. I am so sorry, Honey."

The reason Steven Hyatt was expressing his regrets to me was that I had invested a lot of money in the film he had directed, which had been scheduled to open in New York next week.

The news was a real shock. "What are you going to do, Steven?"

"Well, I'm going back to Australia and shoot

another couple of scenes. I think I can fix this," he answered, and I could imagine him running his bony hand through his wiry brown hair, dislodging his glasses with the gesture.

"What? And not have the dingo dogs eat the survivors?"

Steven sighed into the phone. "I know. I know. That part always bothered you. Okay, you're right and I'm wrong. But I can fix it, honestly. It's just a matter of looking at the scene with another angle in mind."

"I trust you," I said quickly. Steven could get so depressed without encouragement. "When are you leaving?"

"Tomorrow. The sooner the better, and the time window is right. I can get the principals back for a quick shoot if I go now. I'll write the new ending on the plane. I should have it in the can by end of next week."

I kept up the encouraging. "Well, that sounds wonderful. Just a little glitch and delay. No big problem."

"Well, as a matter of fact, there is. Honey, I hate to ask you, but do you think you can advance me another couple of hundred K?

"I would love to, Steven. You know that. But I can't." I hated saying that to him.

"I understand, and I don't blame you. You've

already given me too much. Don't worry. I'll figure out how to get the additional backing. Somehow."

Janie had been standing by my side. She nudged
me in the arm and said, "Ask him for some
money."

I put my hand over the phone. "Hush, I can't.
He's asking me for some."

She raised her eyebrows in a question mark.
"Oh? Well, it was a thought."

I said into the phone, "Steven, its not that. I
would love to give you the money, but . . ."

"Honey, it's okay. And I'll get by. And you're
right. It's time I stood on my own two feet," was
his reply that interrupted my explanation.

Well, now, that part was true. Steven had a habit
of loping through life like a bunny across the
fields. Whatever he found in his journeys he used
and enjoyed and then hopped off to another adventure and opportunity. He kept telling me I
needed to grow up, settle down. Maybe it was time
the shoe was on his foot.

I swallowed my original retort and said, "Well,
I wish you all the luck in the world, you know
that."

"Yeah. And Honey, you know I love you."

This declaration of love and affection from
Steven Hyatt was a recent development. We had

been friends for so long. It was still hard for me to realize that he cared for me in a new way. I was still sorting it out, but I just said, "Yes, Steven. And I love you, too." And I did. I just didn't know which kind of love.

Steven was still talking. "I know that you've been involved with Harry for a long time, and that he wants to marry you. And I like Harry and all. It's just that when I realized that you might marry him that I got to thinking. That's when I knew that I loved you and wanted to marry you. I don't want to lose you, Honey."

Now it was my turn to say, "I know. I know. I haven't gone anywhere. I'm not lost. I'm right here. And I haven't made up my mind about anything. Actually, that's a little hard to do, anyway. Harry is still in England. I think. Steven, no matter what my answer to you is, I have to see Harry first."

"That's only fair," he responded.

"Anyway, nothing will happen while you're in Australia. I promise you that."

"I love you, Honey," he said again. "And I've got to go. Plans to make and miles to cover. Remember, *'Success is failure turned inside out . . .'* "

Now that was more like it; Steven was playing our poet game. "Right, and *'It's when things seem worst that You Mustn't Quit.'* Good luck, sweetie," I said, and I meant it.

I hung up the phone, and Janie pounced on me with questions. "What on earth happened to Steven? Why was he asking for money? Why didn't you tell him about Steven Bondesky's disappearance?

"Hold on. He's had a setback in his movie release, but he's on his way to Australia to fix it. And he wanted more money for the extra expense. I didn't tell him about our financial problems because there is nothing he can do about it, and I didn't want to worry him while he was on location."

Janie said, "Oh, my," as she took in the information.

Then she asked, "What about the other key? Where did you say you found it? What's it to?"

I remembered the keys I held tightly in my fist, their sharp edges making a red imprint in my palm. "In Bondesky's office. In a special file with my name on it."

"Is it the same as the other one?" she asked.

"No. No, they don't match, except that they are both brass keys. And now I've forgotten which is which."

Six

We sat at my dining room table and tried to sort it all out.

"Bottom line," said Janie. "How much money—how much cash—do we have?"

"Bottom line, I have about two thousand dollars in cash. Oh, and twelve dollars and change in my purse. I know that will cover the utilities and get us through the grocery store checkout line. But for how long?"

"Hopefully," she replied, "long enough to find Steven Bondesky."

"Right, but what if we do find him, and there is still no money?"

"Hmm, maybe you shouldn't have quit your job?"

I had. Quit, that is. Several weeks ago. When things were going well, and I had planned to travel. I hadn't wanted to leave my employer, Constant Books, out on a limb while I chased through England looking for the lost Harry. Someone else had already taken on my book route through south Texas. I had tried staying on for awhile, becoming Constant Books' computer liaison between the company's inventory and small, local bookstores that were just beginning to set up computerized systems. I had enjoyed the work but still didn't think it was fair to stay on if I was planning to be gone so much.

And of course, *then* I had the money. The four million dollars.

"If I hadn't insisted you get that money out of the house, we'd still be okay," said Janie ruefully.

"No, you were right. No one should keep four million dollars in their upright piano." I tried to joke. "Not if they're planning a concert career, anyway."

Janie shook her head. "You found the money in the house. It should have stayed in the house. And it's not like you can even play chopsticks."

"This isn't getting us anywhere. Where's that list?" I asked.

"Here." And Janie moved her notebook to expose the written suggestions we had agreed upon.

"First, we call Silas Sampson at the police station and report Bondesky's absence."

"Let's wait on that one, Janie. When I was there, I found I could get into Bondesky's computer. I want to check what I can while the office is still 'open.' "

"Okay, next is find Evelyn Potter. I know she's missing, too, but I can't fathom them—Steven Bondesky and her—together."

"I can. Evelyn had designs on Bondesky from the start."

"Poor choice for her, I'd say." Janie shook her head at the image of the grizzly accountant with the immaculate secretary.

I pointed to Evelyn's name on the list. "At least I know where I can start looking for her. I'm sure if she's not with Bondesky, she's in the Hill Country with Kantor."

"Honey, you're getting so good at this. Of course, Kantor."

Kantor was the older gentleman who had relinquished his book rep route to an untried, green English major fresh out of college: me.

Before he had turned me loose on his precious customers—mostly small-town, local bookstore owners—he had given me a lesson on bookselling and on life. The love of independent bookstores and their devoted owners that I possessed came from Kantor's respect and friendship with them. He had tried hard—and successfully—to instill that same respect and affection for his work in me before he had given up his job at Constant Books to build a prefab cabin deep in Texas's Hill Country, a dream of his come true. That's what he said, but in actuality, he was afraid of the computer explosion that had hit the publishing industry.

I had recently invited my former mentor to join me in Jacksboro, Texas, when I had converted a small bookstore to a computer inventory system. Evelyn Potter had really been the ramrod of the work group I assembled for the job. Computer-shy though he was, Kantor had had the good nature to attend, and an interesting relationship had developed between him and the older but sexy secretary.

"Maybe she's teaching him how to compute," I told Janie.

She put a check mark after Evelyn Potter's name. "Okay, I'll try to reach her at Kantor's. I've already tried her home. No answer. What else?"

"There's these two keys. Now, we know one came for Bailey, so we've got to figure that it was from someone who knows him."

Janie's eyes widened. "Harry, you think?"

"Possibly. We know Bailey went berserk when he smelled the envelope and the key. So, yes, possibly from Harry. Let's see what he thinks now. Here, Bailey," I called.

The Lab didn't have far to go. He got up from his resting position at my feet and shuffled over. I held out the two keys for him to sniff, but he just licked my hand and gave me a questioning look. "It's too late," I said. "Whatever smell was on the keys is gone. I've handled them too much."

Janie defended the dog. "Well, there was that initial reaction. We can't forget that. Yes, I like the idea that the key that came in the mail was from Harry. I wish Bailey hadn't eaten the envelope though."

"I looked at the envelope pretty carefully this morning. I don't think it would have told us anything anyway." I patted Bailey's head to show him it was all right that he had eaten a clue. He just sighed a heavy sigh and lay back down at my feet.

Bailey wasn't my dog. Not really. When my friend, customer, and lover, Harry Armstead, had left for England a couple of months ago, he had shipped the Labrador from his home on South Padre Island to me in Fort Worth. He'd closed his bookstore, Sandscript, on the island and just enclosed a quick note and Bailey's records with the crate that was ultimately delivered to my house by a taxi.

Just as I had become accustomed to having my

friend Janie living with me, I had become fond of the dog who was never far from my sight and who shared a pillow with me at night.

"So, if the key is from Harry, what's it to? What does it unlock?" Janie asked.

"Well, the only place I know that Harry knows is the bookstore on Padre Island. I'm betting it's to Sandscript."

"I thought you already had a key to Sandscript."

"No. Oh, Harry wanted to give me one, but it seemed too personal," I replied.

She stared at me, "You two were lovers for several years, and a key to his bookstore was too personal?"

"It was his *home* too," I said defensively. I'm not as weird in my actions and reasons now as I was then. Suddenly it seemed a silly thing for me not to have accepted the offer of a key. I've come a long way.

Janie shrugged. "Okay, but now we do have the key. So I guess this means we go to Padre and see what's there?"

"Maybe," I mused. "What I can't figure out is why a similar key was in Bondesky's files. I have a feeling the two are connected somehow."

Janie suddenly screamed. It wasn't the same scream she uses when she sees a dead body, but it was enough to startle both me and the dog at my feet. "What? What?"

"I've just remembered an asset we have. Those plane tickets to New York and London. Can we cash them in?"

"I've already thought of that. They're nonrefundable. We do have those English pounds though. About four thousand dollars' worth. They're in that lock box with our passports. Guess I could reexchange them and get dollars."

"Or . . ." and Janie's eyes lit up. "We could use them and go to England. Of course, we'll have to go to Padre Island first to find out what we're supposed to be finding there."

I protested, "Oh, Janie I don't think so."

"Why not? We can be broke and starve in England just as well as we can here."

Seven

Janie Bridges was a plump fifty something who had problems of her own. She had unexpectedly left her husband and moved in with me a few months ago. It was at the same time I was letting down barriers in my life—mainly my self-imposed isolation in my house. I live in a three-story Victorian house slap-dab in the middle of a medical complex. It wasn't a planned community but rather a matter of squatter's rights.

My house was there first.

Janie was in love with the house. She especially liked my mother's bedroom, which she had appropriated as her own. The high oak head- and footboards of the bed and the white, starched eyelet covers appealed to her whimsical sense—the same

sense that made her love a good mystery whether
it was in a book or in real life. Most times I felt
as if I was the older woman, repeating cautions
and adages, which Janie loved, saying they were
directly descended from my mother's mouth.
Which was true.

Taking our *to-do* list upstairs with me, I told
Janie, "I need to take a bath before I start following this list. I think I'll start with the electric company."

Janie giggled as she followed me up the stairs.
"Better make it the water company then. No water,
remember?"

"Oh, shoot. How could I forget? Okay, no bath,
but I sure need one. I was nervous as a pig over
at Bondesky's. I'm sure I smell like one."

Following me into my bedroom, Janie said,
"You know, we got so sidetracked with the bills
and the keys that I forgot all about Mr. Bondesky.
Now, how come you didn't try to read his computer files while you were there?"

I had deliberately avoided telling Janie about
Sledge Hamra. Once she found out I had met a
real private investigator, she would be asking why
I hadn't asked him to supper so she could pump
him for insider information about the investigating
business.

"Thank God for Wet Ones," I said as I pulled

a box from my bedside drawer. "At least I can freshen up before I head out."

Janie cocked her head and her muddy-rainbow bobbed hair, ranging from hues of dark brown to silver gray, fell across her eyes. She pushed the hair out of her face and said, "Honey, you haven't answered my question."

"Oh, all right. There was a man there. A very disagreeable man, I might add. He is a private investigator and is looking for Bondesky, too."

"A PI? You met a real PI? Why on earth didn't you say so? And what is he looking for Bondesky for? Is that why Mr. Pondesky is gone? Aha. He's done something illegal, right? Ran away with all your money and someone else's, too."

I held up my hand, waving the Wet One in the air. "Whoa. Hold on there, Bessie. Before you reach the finish line, may I remind you that you're the one who assured me Bondesky was all above-board in his dealings? And that my money was perfectly safe with him? Not that I am blaming you, Janie, but you are jumping to conclusions here."

"Then why the PI?"

"Mr. Alvin 'Sledge' Hamra is looking for Steven Bondesky because Bondesky handled his finances, too. He seemed as strapped as we are." I threw the used Wet One in the pink trash can by my bed. "Well, I'm off to make the rounds."

"Start at Kroger's," Janie told me.

"The grocery store? I'm paying utilities, not buying groceries."

Janie nodded as she trailed after me as I went downstairs. "Yes, their community desk. You can pay most of them there. All of them, I think."

"No kidding? Well, will wonders never cease. What a convenience. And I didn't check Bondesky's computer files with Mr. Pie looking over my shoulder. Just because he *said* he was looking for Bondesky for personal reasons, how do I know he was telling the truth?" I went into the kitchen to get my purse.

Janie remained on the landing at the bottom of the stairs. She called after me, "Is he seven feet tall and looks like Mr. Clean and dresses like Kramer on the Seinfield show?"

"Yes, that's him exactly. Did I tell you that?"

"No, he's standing on our front porch. Does he always have that angry look on his face?"

We both peered through the lace curtain covering the glass front door. "I don't know," I admitted. "That may be his natural expression. It's the same one he had at Bondesky's. Isn't he awful?"

"I don't know. I think he's kind of cute."

I gave her a disgusted look as I opened the front door. "Honestly, Janie."

Sledge Hamra was reaching for the doorbell key. "Hello," I said. "That didn't take you long."

"I had to stop for gas." Hamra went ahead and turned the key to the doorbell. "Sorry, I've always wondered how those sounded."

I didn't reply.

"Can I come in? I've been thinking about our mutual predicament and have an offer for you."

I looked at Janie. "Is it okay with you? I'm not scared of him."

She nodded her head. "I'm not scared of him."

"Okay, you can come in. But make it quick. I have to go to the grocery store. This is my friend and housemate, Janie Bridges. Janie, Mr. Hamra."

Hamra gave the first smile I had ever seen on his face and reached for Janie's hand. "Pleased to meet you, Miss Bridges."

"Likewise, Mr. Hamra. Would you like a Coke? We still have some cold ones in the refrigerator. I haven't opened the door much. Well, they won't be ice cold, but . . ."

"That would fine, yes. So, you've had your electricity turned off?" He turned from Janie to ask me.

"Temporarily. That's where I'm going. To get it turned back on. As well as the water and hopefully to pay the telephone bill before they cut it off, too." I waved him into the living room and indicated he should sit down on the sofa.

The big man just stood in awe as he gave the room the once over. I'll admit the floor-to-ceiling dark paneled doors that also were on the other wall that opened into the dining room were magnificent and impressive, but I didn't think the velvet-covered furniture with tatted doilies was his cup of tea. He sat down gingerly on the sofa, as if he was afraid it wouldn't hold his bulk. I had my doubts, too.

"What a house," he said. "Lady, you must be loaded. I had that feeling when I saw you at Bond-esky's. Especially when you drove off in that new Plymouth Voyager. That's why I came up with this idea."

"What idea is that?" asked Janie for me as she came in the living room with a tray full of Cokes and tea cookies.

I was surprised that Hamra had such good manners. It didn't go with his looks. He thanked Janie, took a napkin, and then the Coke and a few cookies from the tray. "It's like this. We've both got the same problem. Finding Steven Bondesky and, consequently, our money."

"True," I agreed.

"So, it's clear to me," he said.

"Clear to me," echoed Janie.

"Why am I the one in the dark here? Janie, can I have a Coke, too?"

"Oh, sorry, Honey." She handed me the tray.

"Gee, thanks. Okay, what do you two know that I don't?"

Janie opened her Coke and said, "Why, Mr. Hamra is a private investigator, Honey."

"Right."

"We hire him to find Steven Bondesky. What could be clearer than that?"

"You've got to be kidding."

Janie shook her head. "No."

Hamra shook his bald head. "No."

Janie got up and took the Coke can out of my hand. "Honey, you better run along and pay the bills so we can have the lights on before dark. And the water, so I can cook." She turned to the private investigator perched on the edge of my great aunt's couch. "Mr. Hamra, surely you'll stay for supper?"

Eight

It was a muggy day that turned into a muggier early evening as I drove through the heavy air to Steven Bondesky's west side office for the second time that day. The threat of imminent rain was as clear as the bankruptcy I was going to have to declare if I didn't find the dear man. In fact, the dark clouds overhead contributed to the gathering gloom as much as the early fall sunset.

I didn't know how to do what Sledge Hamra had done to get in the office, so I just used my emergency key. The one Steven Bondesky had given me in case something ever happened. It was to be used for an unspecified occasion, and I figured now was the time. I hadn't wanted Mr. Hamra to know I had the key, and even now, as I fit it in the lock, I turned and looked over my shoulder at the quiet neighborhood.

The first bolt of lightning and resulting thunder sent me scurrying inside the office building. Hard rain began to fall as I closed the door behind me and surveyed the still—I hoped—empty office.

I shut the door to the reception room and hurried to pull the curtains over Bondesky's one outside window before I switched on the overhead light.

One press of my thumb was all it took to activate the silent computer. Quickly I gave the *Clover* password and watched as the screen began to fill with rows of files. I clicked on Client List and was scrolling to the Hs when my eye caught a name that stood out like a neon sign: **Harrison Armstead**.

My Harry.

I again moved the mouse and clicked on Harry's name. Just as it came up, there was a tremendous clap of thunder and the whole room blinked and the computer shut off. I knew Bondesky had surge protectors—he had certainly warned me about them enough—so I waited a few minutes and pushed the On button again.

The computer didn't respond, but the telephone rang.

Without the benefit of a caller ID, I didn't know what to do. Answer or not answer? Suddenly, I remembered that Janie knew I was at Bondesky's office. What if something had happened at the house? I took a deep breath and answered the phone, but it was a tentative "Hello" at best.

"Huckleberry?" Steven Bondesky's gravely voice was unmistakable.

"Bondesky?" I replied in kind.

"What are you doing at my office? I did call my office, didn't I?"

I nodded. "Yes, well . . . you were gone, you know. And I was worried about you and why my bills weren't paid . . ."

He cut me off. "Listen, I don't have much time. Is anyone else there with you?"

I looked around the office. "No. Just me." I added, "Bondesky, are you all right? Where are you?"

"It's not like they're making me stay, you know," he said.

"No, of course not," I answered. "But, who is they?"

There was some static on the line, then ". . . about the money."

"Yes, yes." I said excitedly. "Tell me about the money."

Three things happened then.

Bondesky said, "Oh, no."

Lightning struck nearby, and the line went dead.

The lights in the office didn't even blink as they went to black.

I groped my way to the curtained window. It was only marginally lighter outside when I thrust the curtain aside, and most of the light came from lightning flashes. Something nearby must have been struck. As far as I could see, there was only darkness and blowing rain.

As I drove home in the rain, I thought of another cryptic phone call I had received earlier in the year. A call that had led me down some strange and dangerous paths. *That* call had been from a Steven, too. I tried to look on the positive side. At the end of the first Steven phone call, I had found my four million dollars. Maybe I could refind it if I concentrated on the latest call. My mind totally refused to recall the dead bodies that had accompanied the ensuing melee.

The lights were out on the south side of Fort Worth, too. That is, they were out in my house.

"The lady at Kroger's was glad to take my money, all right," I told Janie and Hamra as we ate Taco Bell salads by candlelight. "But she said it would be tomorrow before the utilities would be reconnected. Do you *know* what they charge to reconnect electricity? It's highway robbery."

Hamra tried to slip Bailey a broken piece of his taco shell. I caught the movement in the glimmer of light and rebuked the big man. "We don't feed Bailey from the table. He has his own diet and own eating vessels on the back porch."

"Sorry," Hamra said, but I noticed Bailey gulped down the meat-laden chip anyway.

Words cannot begin to describe how I had felt when Bailey had fallen on Hamra like a long-lost relative. Disgust and betrayal were just a few that came to mind. "No, honest, I've never seen this dog before," the investigator had denied when I accused him of being an impostor. "Dogs just like me. Always have."

"Sit, Bailey," I commanded the dog.

And he did.

"Hey, good trick. Can he do this one? Down, Bailey."

And Bailey lay down.

"My personal favorite," I said in one-upmanship is 'Dance, Bailey.' "

And the happy dog rose on his back legs and crossed his front paws and "danced."

With a gleam in his untrustworthy eyes, Hamra said, "You're a dead dog, Bailey." And the damned dog fell to a flop on the floor.

"I didn't know he knew how to do that! How did you know? Did you teach it to him? You can get up now, Bailey."

"Yeah, while you were messing with supper, Bailey and I had a little fun. Yeah, I just taught it to him."

"Well, he's a smart dog, yes, but let's cut to the chase, Mr. Hamra. Just who are you, and why on earth should I hire you to find Bondesky?" I wasn't about to tell even Janie that I had heard from the missing man—not with Sledge Hamra still dominating our household.

"Whoa. You do get to it, don't you, Honey?" I didn't even like the way he said my name.

"I'm tired. I find out today I'm broke. What do you want me to do? I've been just about as nice as I can be. Now it's your turn." It was time for the mud to hit the fan. I'm almost thirty years old, and I still can't say the popular vernacular for what actually is supposed to hit the fan. Guess I'll never outgrow my mother's training.

Hamra glanced sideways at Janie and patted Bailey's adoring head before answering, "I am a private investigator. I told you that. I've been away on an assignment—down Mexico way. Actually, I don't even live here. I'm from Arizona, but I had heard about Steven Bondesky and his financial connections. Sometimes I make money that's hard to report." He glanced at Janie again, who nodded at him like she knew what he was talking about.

"Excuse me? You have illegal gains, and you

give them to Bondesky?" I was indignant. Janie
frowned at me, and I remembered we weren't
quite sure where my money had come from, either.
"Go on," I said.

"Not illegal. I earned the money. It's just that
it's mostly always in cash, and the best way to
cover my *gains*, as you put it, is to give it to someone who can . . ." and he hesitated as he looked
for the right word.

"Launder the cash. That's what he means,
Honey." Janie jumped into the conversation. "You
know in your heart that everything Mr. Bondesky
does is not one hundred percent kosher." She
turned to the man on her left. "We understand,
Sledge. What we don't know is where Mr. Bondesky is. Or where Honey's money is."

"Okay, I've got contacts that can help me with
the investigation. With finding your accountant.
What I need from you is information. Like—when
did you last see him, and what was his state of
mind at the time? And has he ever disappeared
before? Did you ever see anyone suspicious hanging around? One other thing: Are we talking really
big money here? That would make a difference,
you know."

Lord, I felt I was betraying my very own flesh,
but I was as worried about Bondesky as I was the
money. I think. Anyway, I answered, "First of all,

there were always suspicious characters hanging around Bondesky, and I saw him last over a month ago, and it was a very emotional event. The funeral of his childhood sweetheart. I helped him spread her ashes, and he was very distracted. Distraught. I've never seen him like that before."

"Ah, now we're getting somewhere. Why didn't you see him after that? I gather you two were close? Closer than just client/accountant relationship? And you didn't tell me how much money." Hamra was good at this.

For the first time today, I started thinking for myself. Questions swirled around in my head. "Let's just say it's a very large amount of money, Mr. Hamra."

Janie yawned. "Can we do this some more in the morning? I'm asleep on my feet. Anyway, we won't find Mr. Bondesky tonight. And tomorrow we'll have lights and gas and, I hope, water. I'll make breakfast, and we can start again." When Janie winds down, she goes out fast.

"Yes, sounds good to me," I said.

Hamra grimaced. "Well, I can't come back, because I have no place to go. I mean it when I say I'm broke. Surely in this big house you have a spare bedroom. Just some place for me to crash? I'm all done in, too."

"There's just three bedrooms, and one of them

is my war room, so, no, we don't have a spare bed," I told him. I was ready for this hulk to go.

"War room?" he asked.

"Honey, there's the top floor. Where Joaquin and Steven Hyatt stayed." Leave it to Janie to spill the beans.

"No. No, he definitely can not stay up there." I said the words, but my mind suddenly zeroed in on one bit of information that had played at the edge of my consciousness ever since I had visited Bondesky's office. If Bondesky had called his office, he had expected someone to answer. I knew it wasn't me, so the question was: Who had Bondesky expected to answer the phone?

Nine

I sat on the low metal stool in the bathroom—the one that had belonged my Great Aunt Eddie and that had been used to capture small soiled garments—and watched Janie do her nightly face-cleansing ritual. As a result of her diligence, her face was smooth and unlined. And all she used was plain old Ponds.

"Why don't you go all around your neck?" I was always hoping for an additional beauty secret because it was no secret that redheads have *that* kind of skin.

"Oh, dear. Are you saying I have wrinkles in the back of my neck? Oh, dear." And she started rubbing double Ponds into the area behind her neck.

"Necks get old, too," I said and realized that was probably not too comforting. I changed the subject, "How on earth could you let that man stay in our upstairs?" I was being generous using the "our."

She avoided answering me with, "Wonder how much that little stool is worth? I bet a lot at the Antique Mart."

"I am not selling my furniture, no matter how broke I get," I said.

"The point I'm making, Honey, is that if Sledge doesn't find Mr. Bondesky, you'll be selling more than an old stool." The liberal application of Ponds also was working its way up into Janie's hairline.

"You think?" I thought. "Yes, you're right, and I'm being stubborn. I don't like that man. I don't trust that man, and I sure don't like him staying upstairs."

"You just don't like it that Bailey took to him so quickly," she said as she finished her face wiping. "And it's not like he can get to us."

Years ago when my father had added the third floor to the house of his maiden aunts, it had been designed to be reached only from the outside stairway. Well, there was one other—secret—way, but I had that one boarded up. My father's premise had been that the aunts were proud that since their father had died, no man had slept under their roof.

Personally, I thought it was a rather sad commentary on their lives, but then again, they had all died before a man had even slept *above* their roof. My mother and father had moved in downstairs, and years later, I was born. My father had used the upper floor for an office/workroom.

"Janie, you know all my father's tools, plans, and invention models are up there. They're all valuable, too."

"I hadn't thought of them," she said with genuine regret. "You want me to go upstairs and tell him to leave?"

"No, its too late now, and besides, you're all greased up for the night." I laughed.

Janie slid a finger across her shiny face. "I usually use a damp cloth to remove the excess, but not tonight. No water. We can take the candle into your room now."

I took the candle I was holding to light the ablutions and led the way into my room. It was usually a festive sight of Laura Ashley pink and green flowers, stripes, and solid combinations. Tonight, with only the candle to illuminate the room, it seemed shadowy and eerie. I settled onto the bed, and Bailey leaped on and curled up beside me. "Traitor," I called him for the umpteenth time that night.

Janie sat in the flowered-upholstered armchair

near the bed and yawned—for the umpteenth time that night. "It's funny how he did that trick for Mr. Hamra. See if he will do it again. For you."

I was dubious, but I pushed Bailey out of the bed and said, "Play dead, Bailey."

Nothing but a tail wag.

"No, he said, 'You're a dead dog, Bailey.' "

"That's an awful thing to say to a dog. Okay. You're a dead dog, Bailey."

And down he went, all four paws straight up in the air.

"Now how do you get him to get up?" Janie yawned again.

"You really should go on to bed," I told her. "Here, Bailey, you little smart doggie, you. Get up here with your mama." Bailey came alive and returned to his nest of pillows beside me on the bed, where he lay with anxious eyes as if he were wondering if we were going to play games again.

"I'm okay. And I do want to hear what happened at Mr. Bondesky's office," she said, her hand covering yet another yawn. "You whispered that you cooked the computer."

"I fried it. Rather, the lightning fried it, but I think I know a way to get it back. That's the only reason I agreed to let Hamra sleep upstairs. Your assignment tomorrow is to keep him busy while I go back to Bondesky's office in the daylight. And you'll never guess whose name I found in the computer before it blew."

"Mine," she guessed.

"I don't know about that. I never got to the Bs. I stopped short when I saw Harrison Armstead in the client file."

"Harry?"

"Yep."

"Our Harry?"

"I assume," I told her. "Right when I clicked the mouse to access his file, the lightning struck. Everything went black. All I wanted to do was get out of there. That's why I have to go back tomorrow, while you entertain Mr. Private Eye Hamra."

"Our Harry! Well, as I live and breathe. What a mystery. All the more reason for us to go to South Padre, I should think. And I did tell you I still couldn't reach Evelyn Potter, didn't I?"

"At her house? Yes, you told me, but I didn't understand your whisper about Kantor."

Janie pointed upward. "We'd better whisper now, too. I keep forgetting we have a guest upstairs."

"What? You don't want to wake him?" I was being sarcastic.

"I don't want him to hear," she said in a lowered voice. "After all, if we spent all evening hissing messages in each other's ears, there's no point in shouting it all out now. And Kantor's answering machine related that he was out in the field doing research. I didn't know he was a botanist, too."

I laughed. "He considers himself a writer now, and his research field is probably a library. I bet he's gone into Austin to do research in the university library."

"He's still working on the Twyman Towerie story?" she asked.

"Yes, that's what he told me when we last spoke. There are already a lot of articles about Twyman and his books, but Kantor is determined to write the definitive book on the late, great Towerie fraud."

"When I think of how close you came to being killed—all because of that man . . ." Janie said and shuddered.

"Hush, it's all over now. Anyway, I bet you a dime that Evelyn is with him. If we do go to Padre, and that's a big *if*, we'll stop by Kantor's place in Fredericksburg and find out what she knows about Bondesky's disappearance. You better go on to bed now, Janie."

She nodded and rose, taking the candle with her. At the door, she paused. "Now, tell me once again. Why is it that we're not calling Silas Sampson at the police station to report that Mr. Bondesky is missing?"

I looked at her ethereal image at the doorway. It would probably give me nightmares all night. "Because," I hissed in my best whisper, "have you forgotten that the last time I reported something about Bondesky to Silas, I accused him of murder? I'm not reporting him to the police again as an embezzler or thief or what have you this time until I know for sure what's up. And besides, remember I told you I spoke to Bondesky on the phone. Although he sounded confused, and that's an understatement, I couldn't really say that he was missing, now, could I? We've got a little experience in this business under our belt now, Janie. We'll figure it out."

I closed my eyes so I wouldn't see the image of her smiling, glowing face over the top of the flickering candle. "Yes," she agreed. "We're getting good at this. And, of course, now we have Sledge's help."

I opened my eyes to see the candlelight flickering off down the short hall. "Oh, right," I said to myself. "Thanks for reminding me. That thought will guarantee a good night's sleep."

Ten

There's nothing like sleeping in a dark, Gothic house through a rollicking thunderstorm to make one want to get up and get started early. And that's not even counting the gory images I had of the stranger in the attic.

I slipped down the stairs in the morning gloom, carefully avoiding those steps that tend to creak your approachment, and silently opened the front door and escaped into the dawn. Not that the precautions seemed necessary. I could hear Janie through the closed entryway doors talking to someone, I presumed Hamra, and smelled the odor of Janie's good coffee. The water was back on—bless the water company. Another deterrent to sleep last night had been the gagging taste of toothpaste rinsed out of my mouth with warm 7UP.

Bailey, I am sure, was wrapped around Mr. Hamra's feet in the dining room. I could pretend that the smart/dumb dog was in on the plan to distract the man while I returned to Bondesky's. The truth—that Bailey liked Hamra a lot—was harder to swallow. I thought dogs had better instincts than that.

Those thoughts and a cup of McDonald's always-hot coffee got me back to the west side for the third time in two days. The computer still refused to respond to my touch, and I put my exigency plan into action.

Although it was still early, I got a first ring answer from Dell Computers in Austin.

"Morning, my name is Honey Huckleberry, and I am a temp secretary for Steven Bondesky. While he was out of town—I'm in Fort Worth—I was attempting to update his files, and I think I have really messed things up on his computer." Sounded legit to me.

And to the tech on the line. "Good morning, Ms. Huckleberry. You've called the right place. What seems to be the trouble, and can you give me Mr. Bondesky's registration number?"

"Where would I find that?" I asked.

With the Dell 1-800 number's live-help technician, I located the registration number and confirmed the request with the string of digits and numbers on the almost-hidden label. Thank heavens that Bondesky had a service contract with Dell.

"Ah, it's coming up now, Ms. Huckleberry. Yes, Steven Bondesky ordered a new Dell Dimension with NT Workstation installed just last spring. Not to worry, this should be a piece of cake."

"I like cake," I joked. "Now what do I do?"

The tech—whose name was Dana—walked me through the recovery process. First eliminating the possibility of lightning strikes, then a systems crash. Words like *reinstall, recovery disc,* and *motherboard* flew over my head, but I just punched the keys and inserted discs like Dana told me to do. Eventually, the computer sprang back from the dead.

"There you go," said Dana. "Piece of cake."

"Before you go, Dana, can you stay on the line while I access the file that I was trying to update?"

"Sure, but I doubt you'll have any problems now," he assured me.

The whole shebang went dead again when I pulled up the Harrison Armstead file.

"Hmmm," said the expert when I explained the problem.

We went through the whole process again, and

this time the computer crashed when I pulled up another file: mine. Then we tried a stranger to me, a Mrs. Robin Aldridge.

Crash.

"Okay."

"Okay, okay. I've got it," said Dana. Lord, he was a patient man. I hoped Dell paid him well.

"I'm all ears," I said.

"You're a temp, right?"

"Yes, Ms. Potter—the regular secretary—is on vacation."

"Okay, we didn't install it here for Mr. Bondesky, but my guess is that he has purchased some of the available software for secondary security, and he didn't give you the password."

I protested, "But I know the password."

"Is Mr. Bondesky's work highly secretive? Like financial numbers? You did say he was an accountant."

"You could say that," I agreed.

"There you have it," he said. "Obviously, he's installed some software that requires a second password. My guess, it's a timed response."

I *didn't* have it. Not the concept or the additional password. "Timed response?"

"Yeah. It's pretty sophisticated for someone not in government work, but you can buy these programs that require an additional password within ... well, whatever time limit you tell it. I'd say yours was about two minutes. Does Mr. Bondesky do some work for the government?"

"You could say that," I agreed again.

"Sorry, I can't help you more, Ms. Huckleberry. Perhaps when Mr. Bondesky checks in or maybe you could locate the regular secretary? And it might just be that they don't want certain files accessed by a temporary secretary. Have a good day," and Dana hung up.

Well, I was up scum pond.

I was surprised at how much time I had spent with Dana and Dell. When I left Bondesky's office, the sun was shining, and it was a fantastic day . . . clear as only a Texas sky can be after a tumultuous, stormy night.

I called Janie from my cell phone.

"Everything's back up," she said. "Lights, gas, water. It's amazing what money can do."

"Where's Hamra?" I asked.

"He left a while ago. I kept him chattering as long as I could. That man tells amazing stories, Honey. He walked Bailey and then left in his truck. Said he had some errands to run."

I'd probably left Bondesky's office in the nick of time. I'm sure it was on Hamra's errand list.

"Well, start packing, Janie," I told her.

"We're going to London?" she squealed.

"No, South Padre Island. We're going to do

some private investigating of our own."

"And I'll be your legs," she said. Whatever that meant.

"Right, and dismantle Bailey's crate. We're taking him with us."

"Honey, what about Sledge?"

"He doesn't get to go," I said.

Eleven

"Tell me some more about Harry," Janie requested as the Plymouth Voyager ate up some of the 500 miles we would have to travel to South Padre Island and *she* made a start on eating up the snacks she had packed for the trip.

"Harry? That's right. You only met him that one time and, of course, with finding Jimmy the Geek dead at the same time you were introduced . . ." I let the sentence trail off.

"I remember he was nice looking, older than you, and . . . hmmm . . . not very tall. Oh, and he had red hair, too—a different shade than yours."

"Yes, more auburn than . . ."

"Orange."

"Right. Orange."

"Or pink."

"Janie, would you quit with the hair?"

She shrugged. "Yours changes color with the light. Right now, it's pink. Gray days make it pinker. It takes the sun to make it that orange color. Want another kolache?" She offered the white bakery box.

"I've had enough," I said and didn't know if I meant of the conversation or the rolls we had picked up at the Czech bakery in West. I turned on the tape player to start up a new books-on-tape package I had in the van. It was an older Grisham, but I hadn't read . . . er . . . heard it. "*The Client,* by John Grisham," said the reader as cassette one, side one, started to play. I recognized the reader's voice, but I would have to check the box for the name. I often listened to books on tape as I rode this highway—my old circuit for Constant Books is as familiar to me as the lines on Harry's face.

Not that he had many lines. Fortyish and in good shape, he'd made a good trim sailor for Her Majesty's Navy. Although I think his rank might have been a wee bit higher than that. I didn't know the British equivalent for Navy SEALs, but I think he told me once he was a commander of one of the units or some such. A nasty injury—accident, he'd said—had sidelined him from his active career, and he'd taken early retirement to roam around the world. A visit to some stateside cousins had led him to South Padre Island and a desire to settle there.

I'd met him when his bookstore, Sandscript, was added to my South Texas route. I'd fallen for his accent, his auburn hair, and his joking manner at the first meeting, but it was several visits later that we became lovers. Being with Harry meant being in fun: spontaneous laughs and meandering moonlit walks on the beach near his bookstore/home.

Though he possessed a superior intelligence, he wasn't serious about his business, his books, or his life. He was serious, however, about his golden Lab, Bailey, and about me. He'd asked me to marry him on my last visit to South Padre and again, on his first and only visit to Fort Worth. That he'd walked into a murder scene only confirmed his intent to take me away to a new life. I hadn't had the time or the heart to answer his question then, and when I finally did have the courage to consider his proposal, he was gone.

When he'd shipped Bailey to me in Fort Worth, the only note he sent was to say he was called home because his mother was ill. Not another word since. Not for months. And now the key addressed to Bailey. It had to be from Harry, and it had to be for the bookstore. Something he wanted me to find in the bookstore. A clue to his whereabouts maybe. And maybe it was tied in with Bondesky's disappearance. I was getting tired of people disappearing on me.

One person I couldn't seem to lose, though, was Sledge Hamra.

The private investigator had met me back at the house while I was still packing the dog crate into the van.

"You skipping out, too?" he'd asked as he walked up to the Plymouth Voyager.

"I was going to leave you a note," I lied.

He stuck his head inside the van, making note of the cooler and luggage. "Like hell you were." Hamra came straight to the point. "Now, do you want me to find Bondesky for you or not?"

Not was my first internal reaction, but an idea clicked into place in my head, and I surprised myself by answering, "Yes, I do. I want to hire you."

My answer surprised the dome-headed man, too. "You do? Well, that's great. I charge two a day and expenses. A special offer to you since I have a stake in this also."

"Two dollars?"

He shook his head and laughed. "Guess again, Honey."

"It better not be two thousand. I can't even afford two dollars."

We started toward the house, and he said, "Look, for you—another special deal. Let me crash in that upstairs, and I'll cut the fee in half." He hung behind me as I sprang up the front steps to the porch.

I considered the risks. It was better, I had surmised, to hire this creep and know where he was at all times—and who knows—he might actually find Bondesky. "Promise me you won't use your key thingy on my house," I said.

"Wouldn't dream of it," he said. And he couldn't resist adding, "I've already been through everything in your house, anyway."

"Braggart," I said to him as we entered the front door just in time to see Janie on the stairs struggling with a bag that seemed to want to stay upstairs while she was trying to wrestle it down. "Help Janie with that bag. And there's a sack in the kitchen that needs loading, too."

Janie dropped the bag just as Hamra reached her. "Honey Huckleberry, how rude. How can you order someone around like that? That's not like you."

"I just hired him. To load bags and find Bondesky," I informed her.

"Oh, in that case, Sledge, there's another bag by my bed upstairs and a case of dog food on the back porch."

"Yes'm, Miss Janie. Anything else I can load for you? Any windows I can do? And by the way, can I inquire where you two ladies are going?"

"Houston," I said while Janie replied, "Corpus Christi."

She changed her destination to Houston while I did mine to Corpus. "Well," I finally said, "Houston for a little business then on to Corpus Christi for a bit of relaxation."

"I thought you didn't have any money," he said.

"We're staying with friends of mine," Janie lied before I could get a chance to do so.

We left Mr. Sledge Hamra standing on my front walk, staring suspiciously at our departing van.

"Bailey," I yelled to the back of the van, "stop your whining. You keep that up one more block, and I'll leave you with the jerk."

Now, miles away from the south side of Fort Worth, I suddenly realized that I hadn't heard a word of the Grisham book. I looked over at Janie. She was out cold. Snoring even.

Bless her heart. It had been hard for her to go back by West, the town about an hour and a half from Fort Worth where she had lived with her husband and had her bookstore, Pages. I had been willing to forgo the customary Czech bakery stop for cream cheese kolaches, but she had insisted. However, she'd waited in the van while I ran in for our to-go order. And also at Pages, the converted gas station where Janie had her business.

"You just go check for mail," she'd said. "I don't have the heart to get out. And besides, the books are probably all collecting dust and that would kill me." Pages was closed while the divorce was pending. Janie owned it, but her husband was asking for half of the value to go against their house. Janie was sure she would get the bookstore, but was thinking of selling it. Small-town bookstores never make money, anyway, and I think she was looking forward to a clean break from West.

I struggled back to the van with a huge box. "It's from Ingram's. It was just sitting outside. Good thing the rain didn't get to it."

Janie came to life. "Oh, I bet it's my back order. I haven't made a regular order in ages. Let's open it."

"Do you have to pay for them if you open it?" I asked.

"Well, yes. If I keep them, that is."

I drove straight to the post office and told the clerk to return to sender.

Needless to say, that made Janie more morose. "We really don't have any money, do we, Honey?"

"Nope, it's getting thin. Cheer up. I have this Grisham tape I haven't heard and I bet you haven't either."

That was hours ago. Now, as I looked at her, Janie stirred and sat up straight. "I missed the start of the book," she cried.

"No problem," I told her. "I'll just start it over."

"It's going to rain again," she observed as she reached back and pulled a diet Coke out of the cooler. "Want one?"

"Sure," I said.

"*The Client*, by John Grisham," said the still un-identified reader, and I drank my Coke and this time listened to cassette one, side one.

Twelve

We were being followed.

I first knew it when we were approaching Austin. Actually, it was a feeling. Over the past few months, I had learned to trust my feelings. They weren't always right, but they were always a harbinger that *something was about to happen.* In between Grisham cassettes, the feeling hit me like a load of bricks. I looked in the rearview mirror and memorized the vehicles behind me. Called myself paranoid as I did so.

Janie doesn't miss a trick. "What?" she asked as soon as I started the traffic inventory.

"Call me paranoid; I certainly am, but would you mind monitoring the traffic behind us?"

"They're going too fast," she declared as she

suddenly realized we weren't the only car on the road.

"Well, yes, but that's a given around here. I meant watch for the other cars and trucks and tell me if they are following us."

Janie laughed. "They're *all* following us ... or we're following them. It's a highway, and we're all heading south." Then she stopped her backward perusal and stared at my grim face. "Oh, my lord, you're serious. Oh my dear Aunt Bessie, is someone after us?"

"Well, if they are, it's not your Aunt Bessie. It's just a feeling I have."

That statement heightened her excitement; she had come to rely on my feelings and hunches. She whipped out her notebook and started making notes. She said her entries aloud as she wrote them down in her particular brand of shorthand. "A green jeep Jimmy, blue Caddie, rusted Ford truck, white Camry, red Chevy station wagon, black Ford truck." Except in shorthand I knew it would come out: gJJ, bCad, rustFtr, wCam, rChwgn, and bFtr.

"How do you know so much about cars?" I asked. I barely knew a van from a bus.

"My husband is an auto dealer. Didn't I tell you that?"

Janie had told me so little about her husband, I didn't even know his first name. I just shook my head and said, "No, you left out that part."

"Well, he is, and that's how I know a van from a bus." Sometimes Janie can read my mind. We took a second to look at each other and grinned. However, now was not the time to discuss cars or husbands.

She bent over her notebook and continued to make out the list, crossing out those who passed us.

"Got 'em?" I asked.

"As well as I can. It's hard to tell in this rain," she replied as her body twisted almost completely around in the seat.

"Okay, now see who does this trick," I told her.

I crossed three lanes of traffic on Highway 35 from the left lane to the right just outside downtown Austin. There is an option for motorists there: to either go straight on the overhead or a right lane for those who want on the express overhead. I didn't close my eyes and cross the three lanes, but I certainly felt like it. I don't recommend the procedure.

"Good Golly, Miss Molly," shrieked Janie. From her vantage point, it must have seemed like I had lost my mind. I know it did to the honking motorists behind me.

Between the good graces of Aunt Bessie and Miss Molly, we safely entered the ramp for the

Austin underground freeway. Traffic was only minimally slower through there, but it was enough so we could tell if anyone had followed my maneuver with the Plymouth Voyager.

"Anyone?" I asked as I watched for traffic.

"The Jeep and the black Ford truck," she answered.

All of a sudden it hit me, "Doesn't Sledge Hamra have a black Ford truck?"

"Yes. Yes. Why didn't I think of that? Let me try to get a look at the driver. Oh, this awful rain. Yes, Honey, it's him. It's him. He has on a gimme cap, but I can tell it's him."

"That dirty dog," I yelled, startling the real dog in the middle seat behind us. Bailey was in a stubborn mood and had refused to lie down between Fort Worth and Austin. He'd stood swaying on all fours despite my frequent admonitions for him to *"Chill out"* and *"Relax."* Not even a harsher *"Lie down"* had fazed him, and he had refused his share of kolaches. This dog was a work of art in passive resistance. Now I told him, "I ought to stop the van right here and let you ride with that idiot behind us."

Bailey circled the pillows in the seat I had put in for his comfort and sat down. It was an improvement, but he still held his majestic snout in the air and pretended he didn't know me.

"What are we going to do?" asked Janie.

"Nothing," I answered. "If he wants to spend his time on the road to Mexico, let him. I know one thing we're not going to do, though."

"And that is . . . ?"

"We're not going to go see Kantor on the trip down. We'll save it for when we return. There's no sense in leading Hamra straight to Evelyn Potter. Let him earn his money and find her himself. Ever seen the Capitol or the university?" I asked her.

Janie had never seen much of anything—never been to Austin, so I took a turn off the underground freeway and drove her by the famous University of Texas bronze horse sculpture/fountain and once around the Capitol grounds.

"He still with us?"

"All the way," Janie said. "What fun this is."

We stopped for gas and then a to-go burger from the Night Hawk. And this time Bailey didn't pass up the chance to eat his own burger. He even lay down on his pillows in the van after I walked him in the grassy area at the gas station. "Finally," I said with relief. I don't know much about dogs, but this one was definitely a challenge.

"That's enough fun for one day," I said. "Let's load 'em up and move 'em out. On to Padre." And I swung back on to 35 South.

"The rain is clearing," said Janie. "I see blue sky up ahead."

"Oh, it's going to be a gorgeous day now. I can just feel it. If you think you liked our little tour of Austin, just wait until you see my Padre."

Thirteen

I chatted away—it was new for me to have company on a trip down into the Rio Grande Valley. Bailey was the better listener.

Janie would rouse from a road-induced stare from time to time to ask something like, "You ever wish one of those new cars would just roll off one of those transport trucks and glide to the side of the road? You know . . . with keys in the ignition and title in the glove compartment?" Or she would nod and say, "There sure is a lot of Texas down this way."

I was telling Bailey about Texas being the second largest grapefruit producing state and was just about to the part where the first grapefruit orchard was planted in the late 1980s when Janie asked out of the blue, "Honey, could you ever kill some-one?"

By the time I had switched mental gears from grapefruit to handguns, she was asking, "I thought you said there were lots of wildflowers on this trip—poppies and wine cups and primroses. All I see is grass or maybe goldenrod."

I turned on the cassette player to another book on tape, a mystery I had heard before but that was new to Janie. I think she listened to it while I explained to Bailey that September wildflowers were not as prolific as those that bloomed in April and May. I also told him that I didn't think I could ever kill someone, and then I backtracked and said, "Well, maybe if someone I loved was in danger, I could—just might could—kill to save the one I loved." And I added the nonsequitor, "Besides, the summer was too hot and dry. If you want flowers, look at the cacti."

In this manner we made our way through a cloudless blue sky to where Texas meets Mexico at the Gulf. I explained to Janie that even if you're running short on money, you still had to stop in Robstown at Cotton's for barbecue, and after her first bite of real Texas chopped beef with onions and pickles, she agreed. "Best thing I've eaten in a month of Sundays," she declared as she let Bailey lick the grease from her fingers. "Even better than the Railhead."

"Only three more hours to South Padre from here. Maybe we'll get there to see the sunset." I told her about Louie's Backyard, where the customers seated on the bay side deck drank margaritas while they waited for the sun to go down. "They always applaud," I told her.

"For a sunset?"

"Wait and see."

Later, she noted, "Are you sure we're going the right way?"

"Yep," I replied. "I know this area like the back of my hand. Why?"

"There are so many cars coming this way. I thought maybe the beach was back that way."

"There are a lot of cars going north, but I reckon they are weekenders heading home."

"It's Wednesday," she said.

"Well, maybe they're taking the kids home for school to start. Schools start at different times in different parts of the country, you know."

"Just seems strange," she said. "Like they know something we don't. I think we're the only ones heading south."

"Except Sledge Hamra," I reminded her. "And I haven't seen his truck behind us in a while."

I was getting so excited. I was in love with South Padre Island long before I met Harry Armstead. I had visited the Sandscript when the older couple—owners before Harry—had owned it. I loved the sea breezes, the fishy Gulf smell, and the endless miles of white Texas sand. I couldn't wait to show it to Janie. She came out of her road lethargy about five miles out of Port Isabel, and by the time the Port Isabel Lighthouse was in view, she was sitting on the edge of her seat, straining to see the sights ahead. I started a running commentary on the area, beginning with the refurbishing of the lighthouse, explaining that's why the top of the lighthouse was off.

"Where do they clean lighthouse tops?" Janie wondered, and we laughed. We were giddy with anticipation. We laughed at the gigantic, sprawling, purple octopus on the shell shop, and I pointed out the yacht club, telling her we would eat there, but we didn't have the money. And we laughed because we had no money. Everything seemed carefree and light. It was a beautiful day.

When we started over the causeway, Bailey started a ritualized whine from the backseat. I knew he smelled the sea air and home.

"I love this bridge," said Janie.

"You ought to see it lit up at night," I told her— still the tour guide. "It looks like a carnival ride. One time Harry rented a boat, and we went under it. Talk about scary."

"Why did they have those barriers back there?

Do they check everyone who comes on the island?"

Confident in my island lore, I explained. "It's the border patrol. They do periodic surprise checks for illegal aliens from Mexico. I've run into them lots of times down here."

"Well, they should keep them manned. I thought you were going over the side of the causeway when you went around those orange cones."

"They probably just went out for coffee . . . or a shrimp sandwich. Oh, Janie, you're gonna love being down here."

I pulled into a parking spot at Louie's just before the sunset. I apologized to Bailey as Janie and I ran to an open area and looked out on the peaceful bay.

"Was it everything I promised?" I asked her.

The evening's sunset was nothing short of spectacular. Even I was amazed. "I've never seen such colors," I told her. We both applauded a final glimpse of the fiery sun ball. Golds, purples, and reds filled the sky. "If you painted this, they would call it a fake," I said.

"There was no one at Louie's Backyard," she said.

"It's a Wednesday, like you said. Sometimes I wonder how these businesses stay open in the off season. Would you just look at all these boarded-up places? They'll reopen when the snow birds get here." And then I had to explain about the Northern retirees who winter on the island to get away from the snow and cold of the upper states.

"They start arriving around Thanksgiving and stay until Easter. The locals take their vacations now. Harry says most them head to Colorado to ski. Aren't people funny?"

We were still in wonderment of the awesome sunset when I drove up to the beach access parking area across the narrow island. This time Bailey accompanied us as we walked across the wooden walkway to the beach. I let him go, and he ran to meet the waves. I was not far behind him, and neither was Janie, who caught on fast. She peeled off her shoes at the water's edge and squealed when the first tiny wave caught her toes.

There was still a lot of light, and we cavorted like kids in the warm surf, not caring that our shorts were soaked to the waist. I laughed and called to her, "Didn't I tell you? Didn't I say it was fantastic?"

Bailey made a fool of himself, and I think he would have cried if he could have. He dove into the waves and swam back to tell me about it. He woofed and squealed as loudly as Janie.

"The water is so warm," she said as she finally just sat down in the shallow waves.

"Yes, this is that time of year. Hurricane season, you know?"

"What's that? I thought you said hurricane something . . . ?"

"Yes," I shouted back over the roar of the surf. "It's when the Gulf waters are still warm and the air is colder up high . . . or something like that. It's over in November." I saw her look nervously around, and I laughed. "Don't worry. They have excellent tracking and warning systems here. Believe me, we'd know if there was a hurricane out there."

"It's as warm as a bathtub," she said, her spirits revived with my assurances.

Then suddenly it was dark.

And *out there* was gray and menacing looking.

"I'm ready to go now," Janie told me, and Bailey came up to me with a questioning look, too.

I retrieved towels from the back of the van, and we rubbed Bailey off and wrapped big colorful beach towels around us before we got in the van.

"And I'm hungry again," Janie said in surprise. "Never thought I would want to eat again after Cotton's."

"Harry always keeps steaks in his freezer. I'll cook them on the deck. No one can see us from there. Remember, we don't want anyone to know we're here." *Especially Sledge Hamra*, I thought as I recalled our road stalker.

The short ride over to the Sandscript was as quiet as the deserted Padre Boulevard. "Everyone's gone to eat," I said. "You should see the restaurants at night here where the customers are as red as the lobsters they eat. You have to use common sense when it comes to fun in the sun."

I got out of the van to try the brass keys in the locked garage behind the bookstore. The first one didn't work. The second turned the lock as if it was greased.

"That answers that," I yelled back at Janie. No sense in being discreet in the vacant street. "The key fits."

"That's just the garage. What about the bookstore? And how will we get into his apartment?" she called out.

"Oh, it's the same key. I remember that. To the door inside the garage." I lifted the garage door that was already wet with the night sea spray and then drove the van inside. "Wait here," I told Janie. "I'll close the garage, and then no one will ever know we're here."

Fourteen

Bailey ran through the door like a chicken with its head cut off. He bounded up the stairs to the living area, and before Janie and I could make it to the top, he had already scouted each of the rooms upstairs. He passed us on a gallop on his way down to the bookstore.

"Bless his heart," Janie said. "He's looking for Harry."

I yelled after the dog, "Bailey, he's not down there, either," but finally I had to go open the bookstore so the Lab could make his own decision. It was several minutes before we could drop our soft-sided luggage on Harry's living room floor. I fell rather than sat in a living room chair, and Bailey came up and put his big golden head on my knee.

"I know. I know. I'm sorry he's not here, too, but we'll find him, I promise."

"He probably needs some water," I told Janie. "Use one of Harry's serving bowls until I can get his dog bowls out of the van."

Janie went into the open kitchen area to get Bailey a drink and said, "Honey, there's his dog bowl here on the floor. I'll just rinse it out and give him a drink. Here, Bailey."

I looked into the kitchen. "That's his food bowl. Just use a serving bowl for the water."

We were both concerned about the morose Lab until he drank some fresh water and sighed and settled down in *his* place by the couch.

"I think we can quit futzing with him now. He seems to accept that Harry is not here." I proceeded to defrost two steaks I found in the freezer. It only took a few minutes in the microwave, and while I rummaged in the pantry for something to accompany the meat, Janie took a quick shower to wash off the sand and salt from our impromptu water outing.

"Do you mind watching the steaks? I decided it would be quicker to cook them on the stove. I'm starved, too. And we can use those tomatoes we bought at the market in Harlingen for a salad. Oh, and I found a can of Ranch Style Beans. There's no bread though."

Still drying her hair with a towel, Janie said, "I saw some Bisquick in the refrigerator. I'm sure it's still good. I'll make up some quick biscuits."

"Hmmm ... sounds delicious. I'll only be a minute." And I went off to Harry's bathroom to take my own hasty shower. I had been grateful for the perpetually air-conditioned apartment when we had arrived from the beach, but I shivered in the cold air as I stepped from the shower. I wrapped myself in Harry's big terry bathrobe hanging on the bathroom door. So far, I had seen no signs that his departure had been unusual or hurried.

Our stomachs got in the way of the reason we were guests in Harry's house, but as we mopped up the last of the bean sauce with the biscuits, I reminded Janie, "Now we've got to concentrate on what it is that Harry expected us to find here."

"I think that was the best meal I've ever had," she said. "And can that wait until the morning? I've never been so tired in my life. I don't even think I can wash up the dishes." Telltale dark circles under her eyes told me that Janie was succumbing to beach life in a hurry.

"Eat, play, sleep, and eat." I laughed. "Welcome to the coast."

Janie tried to stay awake, turning on the television, but giving up in frustration as the programs came across in Spanish. "Do you have to know Spanish to watch TV down here?"

"It's something on the remote control. I can fix it, I think. I've watched Harry do it."

"Never mind. I'm packing it in. They talk so fast and seem so excited. It wears me out." Janie turned off the television and headed for the bedroom. She stopped at the door and cocked her head, "I think the wind's picking up," she said. "Doesn't it sound louder to you?"

"It's always that way down here. You'll get used to it. And that sorta roar you hear in the background? That's the waves. Like my mother always said, 'No matter where you go or where you are, those waves are still coming in.' "

"I suppose that's a comforting thought." She yawned. "But I'm going out! Like a tide. I promise I'll do the dishes first thing tomorrow. Night, Honey."

I snuggled into Harry's favorite chair and drank the remains of my after-dinner coffee. I missed his presence in his house. Seemed I missed him more when I didn't have so much else to think about. It wasn't long before I, too, gave it all up, and Bailey and I crept in next to the gently snoring Janie. Harry's king-sized water bed rolled gently with our motion, and as usual in this bed, I slept like a top. The Gulf wind could howl and scream, but I felt safe and protected, which only goes to show you what I still need to learn in this world.

We slept late, which wasn't a surprise. Ocean air does that to people, but I was startled to find that Janie had woken before me. She appeared by my side with a hot cup of coffee. "Just like I promised. Dishes all done and Bailey's been out. It's such a gray old day out there. I'm disappointed, but I guess storms come in here, too. Just seems like it shouldn't rain when you're on a vacation."

I didn't have the heart to tell her we weren't actually on a vacation. Instead, I reassured her. "I'm sure it will blow out soon, and if we spend the morning looking for whatever clue we're supposed to find, maybe we can spend the afternoon at the beach." As an afterthought, I said, "No one saw you when you took the dog out, did they?"

"There's not a soul around. Just wind and rain. I stood in the garage doorway while he did his business. Believe me, he wasn't out there long."

"Really? Usually he takes forever." I looked at the dog, who cocked his head and whined at me. "Poor baby. He still thinks Harry will show up."

Janie patted Bailey on the head. "Would you listen to that wind! I dreamed all night that people were calling out to me—like through megaphones.

I don't know if I could take those waves pounding all the time." She took a drink from her own coffee cup. "Now, where do we begin?"

Good question.

We started with the bookstore. Janie wanted to see it, anyway, and with the sun-filter shades drawn over the windows, no one could see the light inside. She loved the store and was really into examining Harry's stock. "Lots of mysteries," she noted.

"Mostly beach reading. That's what Harry called it." I stopped in the middle of the store and tried to think like Harry. "Janie, there is something here that Harry wants us to find. Now, what could it be?"

She looked up from the revolving rack she was perusing and said, "Well, it would have to have something to do with Bailey . . . or dogs. I figure that's why he sent the key to Bailey."

"You think? I thought that was just his way of telling me it was from him." I wandered around the store. "Something to do with Bailey. With dogs. He has a small pet section. Over in that corner. We can check it out first. Lord, what a day. Would you listen to that wind?"

We spent some time checking each of the books about dogs, paying special attention to anything that had to do with Labradors, but found nothing of unusual interest. Then Janie got the idea of checking mystery books that were about veterinarians or had a dog sleuth.

Nothing.

She went upstairs and brought down some hot coffee and toasted leftover biscuits. We munched on the breakfast and thought what we could explore next. "The storm is getting worse, Honey. And I saw some emergency vehicles going by with red lights flashing. Reckon we ought to listen to the weather report? Maybe it's a hurricane."

I laughed. "Janie, the last hurricane that came in this late in the season was Beulah back in 1967. I don't think we need to worry, but we'll turn on the TV when we go upstairs. But, first, think. Think of something that would have to do with just Bailey."

"That's not very comforting," she said.

"What?"

"Well, if this Beulah did come in . . . in September, that means another one can, too."

I was sitting on the floor, leaning on the checkout counter. "I've got it," I shrieked.

"You figured out the clue?" Janie forgot all about Beulahs and hurricanes.

"I see one of Bailey's toys under that display. He has them everywhere. We just need to go around and collect them and, well, I bet we find what we're looking for."

It didn't take long to look high and low for Bailey's babies as Harry called them. He had sent some with the dog when he had flown him to Fort Worth to me, but there was still a zoo of stuffed animals and a few balls lying around. We gathered them up and took them back to the living quarters. Bailey thought it was a fine game, and he gave each new discovery a yelp and a lick.

"Look, Bailey, here's monkey and chicky," I told him as I dangled the animals in front of him. He thought it was a game and grabbed them both, tossing them into the air and catching them.

We found another cache upstairs, and soon we were squeezing and examining all the stuffed toys. "Look for any seams that might be loose. Or something unusual."

Janie held up a stuffed shark and said, "They're all unusual." She turned to Bailey, who wanted the shark. "Anyone ever tell you that you are a rotten spoiled dog?" He agreed with her and took the shark out of her hands after a tug.

"Honey, there's nothing in or on these animals. I give up. And Bailey's hungry. I'm going to feed him." She went into the kitchen to get his food. When she came back, she said very quietly, "Have you ever seen the movie *Key Largo*?"

"I don't think so," I replied. "I've meant to, but I don't remember it. Why?"

"Because it was about a hurricane, and I saw it recently. It was all filmed on a set, and I remember thinking how fake the palm trees looked blowing over in the wind. Like someone was pulling them over with wire or something."

"And?" I prompted her to finish.

"Well, I was wrong. That's the way the palms outside look right now. They're almost bending clear to the ground. We forgot to turn on the TV, but I'd bet my bottom dollar we're in the middle of a hurricane."

I jumped up and went to the curtained sliding glass door of Harry's balcony. I pulled aside the dark curtain and gasped. Janie was right. The palms surrounding Harry's bookstore—and all those for as far as I could see—were bowing low to the ground. Rain came down in slanted sheets, and the wind was like a howling monster. The waves in the Gulf were high and angry. I had never seen them so gray and menacing. Or so near the bookstore.

"Oh, my God," I said.

Janie was reaching for the TV remote when the lights went out.

In the dark, the wind seemed to take a life of its own, becoming an unwelcome guest who was determined to come in. The glass shook as a wind shift drove the rain against the pane. I ducked as if something had been thrown at me and dropped the curtain.

Out of the black space where Janie stood, I heard, "Oh, and I found Harry's clue. It was taped to the bottom of Bailey's food bowl."

Fifteen

I didn't know what to do.

Surprisingly, Janie was the calmer one. "Don't panic," she said. "We'll just get in the van and go very slowly back over the bridge."

"Oh, dear," I said.

"What? What's with the 'oh, dear'?"

"I remember something Harry said. The bridge was designed for a car to withstand an eighty-mile-an-hour wind. Hurricane winds begin at about fifty miles an hour, and right now, it sounds more like one hundred miles an hour out there."

We reversed roles, and Janie became the panicked one. "That means we can't get across the causeway?"

"Not in the van. It would blow us over in a New York minute. Let me think."

I didn't want to look out that glass door again, but I raised the curtain and tried to peer through the rain. It was only marginally lighter outside, but I could see that the water was closer to the book- store. I didn't see a light or anything moving as far as I could see.

"It's getting stuffy in here," said Janie. "I can't breathe."

"That's because the air-conditioning is out. You're feeling the humidity. Just stay calm and breathe naturally. I'll figure something out."

"Let's go down to the bookstore so the wind won't blow us away."

"Oh, right, and risk drowning. That storm surge is sure to flood the downstairs."

Janie and Bailey both whined at that one.

"The question is—do we want to drown or be blown away?"

More moans from the two. It was as if even Bailey knew what was going on.

I turned, and in the pale light from the sliding glass door, I could see the two huddled together. Janie was on the floor by the couch with her arms around Bailey. He had his big head buried in her shoulder. "Okay, just joking." I said. "But we have to get a grip. Janie, you look in the kitchen for candles. I know Harry keeps an emergency supply. I'll hold the curtain open for light. I can't find the drawstring. Yes, there—in that drawer. Now see if there are some matches in there. Good. Light them all."

The room took on an eerie glow, but at least we could see our hands in front of our faces again. I ran a mental list of things to do in a hurricane. "Okay, we've got plenty of bottled water. Now I know why they call them hurricane lamps. Just put the glass back on that one and bring it over here." I tried to joke to reassure Janie, but the truth was, I was scared to death. What to do? What to do?

For the minute, we sat on the floor and stared at the candle.

I thought a change of topic would be good while I figured out how to get us rescued. "You said you found the clue? What was it? On Bailey's dish?"

Despite the increasing humidity and oppressive air, Janie replied through chattering teeth, "Yes. It was a note wrapped in tape. This is, what's left of it."

"What do you mean, *what's left of it*? Bailey didn't eat it, did he?

"No, it was this way when I turned it over. A scrap is all I found."

"Did you get to read it? What did it say? Let me see it."

"It didn't make sense. Something about Indians."

"Indians?"

"Well, wigwams or something. Honey, I'm scared. And I don't know what I did with the note."

"I see it on the counter. I'll get it."

"Don't leave me," she shrieked.

"I'm just going to the kitchen to get the note. There, see I'm back, and we're still okay. I see what you mean. It's like the note was ripped off in the middle and the tape held this part. Janie, it doesn't say *wigwam*, it says *wigmore*. 'Honey, Twenty Wigmore St. is for . . .'" And that's it; the rest is gone."

"Wigwam. Wigmore. What difference does it make? We're going to die here."

"And a number. Twenty. Janie, look at this. Does that look like S-T to you? Like in *street*? Or like in *saint*? Well, it has my name on it. This must be what we were looking for."

"Hush," she commanded.

"What? Hush? Why?"

"I hear something."

"I do, too. The wind."

"No, this is from downstairs. Listen. There. Did you hear it? Bailey did."

And sure enough, the dog had cocked his ears toward the downstairs door.

"I don't hear a thing, but we'll go check it out," I said partly to humor her and secretly because I wanted to see if the bookstore had flooded yet.

Janie sprang up and lunged at the door. "I know. They've come to rescue us."

Still trying to lighten the mood, I said as I followed her and the eager dog down the steps, "Maybe it's our friend Sledge Hamra." I had to yell to be heard over the wind. "I bet he got caught here, too."

There was about an inch of water on the bookstore floor. Janie peeled off her sandals at the foot of the stairs and waded into the room. Bailey thought better and stayed where he was on the last step. Water in his home was obviously puzzling to him.

I called out to Janie, "Janie, stop. We don't know *who* it is."

She stopped but said, "Don't be silly. It's the Coast Guard. See? He has a gun."

I blew out the candle I carried.

"Duck down behind that display," I ordered her.

Janie did as I said but still questioned my motives. "Why? We're going to be rescued."

"Rescuers don't come with guns in their hands," I said.

"Maybe they do if they think we are looters. Yes, that's it. They are checking the buildings for looters." She began to stand up again. "Wonder how they will get us off the island?"

"Stay down, and just let me check it out, okay?"

"Do you think they will let us go get our bags? I really don't want to leave my purse." In her mind, we were already safe and sound back on the mainland. But she did stay out of sight while I inched through the water toward the door.

Sure enough, there was a man trying to get in the front door. The closer I got to the door and display windows, the more I could make him out.

"He's not wearing a uniform," I whispered to Janie.

"You don't need to whisper. No one could hear us in here. Not with all that wind. And did you stop to think that maybe when they called him to come do rescue work that he was eating breakfast and didn't have time to change? Or his uniform is at the cleaners?"

Someday, when I have time, I'll have to think about Janie and her convoluted reasoning. Right then, I was more concerned with the man with the shiny gun. He gave up on forcing the door and used the gun to smash in the window above it. I couldn't hear the crash, but I did see glass go flying everywhere. Remembering my bare feet, I drew further back into the store.

"Yoo-hoo, we're in here," yelled Janie.

The man stopped as if he had heard her, which I doubted, but then he looked suddenly over his right shoulder. It was hard to see through the pelting rain, but I thought I saw another figure—seemed to be a big man—approach the other one through the gloom. The water seemed higher outside; the bookstore door must be holding back some of the surge. Both men faced each other and struggled to keep their footing in the swirling water. Neither seemed to be coping well with the weather.

"What's happening?" asked Janie from her concealed spot.

I didn't answer. I was too engrossed in watching the two men begin to struggle with each other. The new man knocked the first man down, and I saw the gun fly out of his hand. It was like watching a boxing match through a grainy filter. The first man tried to get to his feet, but the big man hit him again and again and then actually held him down in the water that whirled around them.

"He's trying to kill him," I said.

"What? What? Can I get up now? What did you say? I can't hear you." Janie complained.

"No," I shouted. "Stay where you are!"

I had looked away to yell at her, and when I looked back, I saw only one person standing. I tried to make out which one it was, but it was just impossible from my position to see clearly through the rain. Then there was a sudden flash of lightning, and the scene was brilliantly lit for a mere second.

I gasped through the muggy air in astonishment.

"Would you please tell me what's going on?" Janie sounded almost in tears.

What was I going to tell her?

What I said was, "I think we're really being rescued this time. There's some kind of truck with a flashing red light heading this way."

"What about the man?"

"He's gone," I said.

I didn't feel like explaining that I thought I had just seen one person kill another and that in that last flash of lightning, I thought I had seen our friend Sledge Hamra standing and staring at the bookstore.

I said again—to reassure myself as well as her, "Whoever it was, he's gone."

Sixteen

They did let us go back and get our purses, but nothing else.

It was definitely a surreal feeling to step from water to the steps going up to the apartment. All the way across the bookstore, I kept thinking, "There is water here. There shouldn't be *water* here." Guess I was in a little shock also.

I didn't know how to answer the officer's question of "is there anyone else here?" Janie told him that someone else had been seen outside, but he wasn't with our family. All I could manage to say was, "He fell in the water."

The first officer's companion in the emergency truck—some kind of fire truck—began a cursory search of the immediate surroundings, shining his huge torch light in the black water. He must have seen something because by the time Janie, Bailey, and I were perched in the high cab of the fire truck, another vehicle had arrived, and its occupants were gathered around something in the surf.

"Why aren't we going?" asked Janie.

One of the new arrivals, a Coast Guard officer, answered her by sticking his head inside the fire truck and yelling to be heard over the wind. "Can one of you come back and identify this man?"

Janie and I looked at each other. "Well, we can't very well send Bailey," she said, and she made as if to follow the officer.

I put up my arm to restrain her. "You always scream when you see dead people. Let me go.

"We'll both go. Stay, Bailey."

I couldn't tell if the storm was any worse, but if the sound was an indicator, we were still in Mother Nature's war zone. Coast Guard personnel held on to each of us as we crossed the few yards to where a body lay in the knee-high water.

In real-life scenarios, even the police are not supposed to touch a body, but what with the way the current was pulling at the still form, it was no big deal for the guard to turn the body over so we could see it. He shined a flashlight into the deceased's face. "Know him?" he shouted.

It was worse than looking at Janie's Ponds-greased face in the candlelight at home. I now had a new image to haunt my dreams. Any natural color the man had possessed had faded, replaced by an iridescent glow of pasty white and mottled shadow. Other than that, he looked like an ordinary tourist or resident.

If Janie screamed, I thankfully didn't hear it, but I did see her yell into one of the Coast Guardsman's ears. He waded over to me. "She says she's never seen him. What about you? She said he might be the man who was trying to find refuge in the bookstore."

I forced myself to look at the dead man again. "Could be. I didn't get a good look at him, but he's about the right size. I don't know him. There's something familiar about him, but I don't know him. How did he die?"

"There's a gash on his head. We think he was hit by flying debris—these winds are killers—and then drowned when he fell."

Our respective escorts maneuvered us back to the fire truck. Those same killer winds were still tossing lethal-sized missiles at us, and there was nothing more we could do for the dead stranger. As we finally began to drive away from the bookstore—into what looked like straight into the ocean to me—I looked through one of the small windows of the cab. I was trying to see if any of the lightning flashes illuminated the bald head of my very own private investigator. All I could see was acres of dirty surf and tall palms paying obeisance to the wind.

At the South Padre Island Convention Center, chaos reigned. The huge cinder-block complex sprawled at the north end of the bay was full to overflowing with "damned stupid people," according to our fire truck driver. "Don't you people ever listen to the television? The radio? We've been forecasting this hurricane for three days."

"We were listening to books on tape," said Janie.

There were church-sized tables lined up at the door of a large room—presumably a convention showroom or auditorium—and the lines in front of it were moving swiftly. We joined the line at one table behind two very red men.

"We're Canadians," said one of them. "Got a bit more sun than we bargained for and have been out drunk since then, trying to ease the pain. You have anything for sunburn?"

I could testify to the drunken part. Even standing a few feet behind them, I could smell the leftover residue of quantities of rum and coconut juice. It was all I could do not to retch at the smell. I pulled the blanket the Coast Guard had given me closer around my shoulders as the men in front of me loosened theirs to show their burnt bodies. One of the women rose and escorted them away to a first-aid station.

We were next.

We gave names and addresses and reported no injuries. To my surprise, the person at the make-shift desk told me we owed two hundred dollars.

"For picking us up in the fire truck? I thought that was a free service."

"For ignoring the hurricane warnings. The fine is one hundred dollars a day, and since you said you arrived yesterday, the fine is two hundred dollars. I still don't understand how you got through the barriers at the bridge."

"Do you take Visa?"

They did, but Visa didn't take us. My credit had been cut off due to my being behind in payments. I saw two hundred dollars of my dwindling cash reserve cross over the Coast Guard's desk.

"When will it be safe to leave?" I asked.

"We'll let you know. Probably tomorrow morning. This thing is dying down fast. The National Guard and Red Cross will take over tomorrow if it clears out. They'll tell you when you can return to your home. Next."

Since we had a dog with us, we were eventually assigned to a separate room. Which didn't make sense to me. Why put someone with a dog into a room with other dogs? I kept a tight hold on Bailey's leash as the canine residents of the smaller room welcomed him with growls and barks.

Janie didn't seem to notice. "I'm wet and cold," she complained.

"That's because the air conditioning is working here. They must have an auxiliary power system. And you're wet because you've just waded into the middle of the Gulf of Mexico. Sit here in this corner with Bailey, and I'll go find us some coffee. I think it's free."

Janie called after me, "Do you think we'll have to pay the National Guard, too?"

Back in the main room, more people seemed to be pouring in from the outside. I wandered around looking for coffee and Sledge Hamra. At the coffeepot a man behind me said, "We're very lucky."

"Yes," I replied grudgingly. "They've done a good job here."

"No, I meant about the hurricane. Charley it's called. Hurricane Charley. Most of it hit Mexico. We're only getting the outer edge of it."

"I bet Mexico doesn't feel so lucky," I told him as I filled two Styrofoam cups.

"I knew it was going to hit Mexico. That's why I stayed. What a glorious sight it's been. If it weren't for the Coast Guard, I'd still be at my condo watching it. We were safe. Don't know why they made us come down here."

Three small kids ran up to the man. They were wet and shivering in the cooled air. "Daddy, I want to go home," cried one.

"Let me drink this coffee, and I'll figure out a way to sneak us out of here," he told them as they wandered off.

"Fool," I muttered. It was one thing to be an unknowing fool—like I had been—but it was another to risk your life and more importantly, your children's lives on a thrill-seeking binge. All of a sudden I didn't resent the two-hundred-dollar charge. How much was life worth, anyway? Seemed cheap to me.

"It'll be over soon," a woman said to me as I took the coffee back to the dog room. "They say the winds are dying down."

"We're lucky," said another stranger. "If the hurricane had stalled offshore, we'd have been in more trouble. Higher tides and more wind."

A woman with a Coast Guard band on her arm passed by and said, "Yes, Charley is almost a category four, but the eye hit Mexico. And she's come in fast and clean."

"It'll be over by morning," predicted another.

Someone in the corner turned on a boom box, and country music blared from the speakers. No one seemed to mind.

Eventually I found my way back to Janie. I had

made the rounds of all the groups in the main area, and unless they had a special room for bald-headed men, Sledge Hamra was not in the building.

"We're lucky," I reported to Janie.

Seventeen

"So why do you they call the hurricane Charley and then refer to it as *she?*"

"All hurricanes used to be feminine names, and that made women mad, so now they alternate. One woman name. One male name. They started this year with Art, so it was time for another guy's name. But they're all *shes*. Like *she's* offshore. Or *she's* packing high winds.

"Well, I'm glad to see the end of *she*," laughed Janie.

"Amen."

"You've still got some of that dog stuff on your sandal," she told me.

"I imagine I'll be buried with it somewhere on

my body. Who knew dog food would swell up in water like that?"

"Or multiply?" Janie added.

Harry's garage had been swimming in the stuff. The force of the water in the garage had overturned the metal trash can he used to store Bailey's food, and the resulting mess was like dog doo without having the benefit of being processed through the dog. It was bad enough when the garage floor was covered with a foot or more of water, but as the water receded, it became like sliding on mud.

"Are you sure that was all just from one can?" Janie had asked.

"Bailey, you will not eat that," and I jerked on his leash as he bent his head into the mess.

Janie started taking off her sandals.

"What do you think you're doing?"

"Well, one of us has to see if the van will still start. It might as well be me."

I always think I have to guard Janie and be the hero. I don't know why that is. I think it's left over from my overprotected childhood. And most of the time I certainly considered Janie to be younger than I was and therefore in need of protection. This was not one of those times. I crossed my arms over my chest and sat down on the last dry step in the stairwell. "Okay."

She slipped on the first step and came up with a body armor of slimy dog food. "I can't get in the van this way," she cried.

"If you make it to the door, take off your clothes," I suggested calmly.

So that's why Janie was sitting in the driver's seat of the Plymouth Voyager in her bra and panties when the representatives of the Red Cross and FEMA came visiting. To their credit, they pretended like nothing was out of the ordinary. "We just need to know if you need any assistance," the younger of the two men said.

Janie reached back and grabbed a sandy towel from the middle seat. She wrapped it around her as she responded. "You could wait and see if the van starts. And as for anything else, you can ask her. She's Harry Armstead's fiancée."

I didn't bat an eye.

The men were local representatives and knew Harry and Bailey. They acted like our being in Harry's apartment was nothing out of the ordinary. One of them—the soft-spoken Hispanic one—even said he had seen me eating out with Harry at Blackbeard's.

I told them that Harry was out of the country visiting his sick mother. And did they know how to get in touch with Rosa, the woman who cleaned for Harry and haphazardly ran the bookstore when he was gone? They said it would be no problem to find her, and we all were relieved when we heard the engine turn over in the van. Janie gave a thumbs-up from the front window.

"The National Guard is opening the causeway this afternoon. You can leave whenever you want to, but what about the cleanup here?"

"I'm sure Rosa will know what to do," I said confidently. "I'd have you take her some money, but I'm broke."

They raised their eyebrows on that one but soon left, assuring us that they would watch out for looters and strangers at the bookstore. They also told us as they departed that there was still no identification for the victim found dead outside the bookstore, but that they would let us know if they found out who he was. The authorities were sending the corpse's body to Austin to check for fingerprints and dental records. I still didn't mention the gun or seeing who I thought was Sledge Hamra attacking the dead man. I hadn't said a word about Hamra to Janie, either. As the hours passed, it seemed more unlikely that I had seen our Mr. Clean in the middle of Hurricane Charley.

Janie struggled back through the goo, the beach towel wrapped around her middle held with one hand and clutching a gunky mess of clothes in the other.

"They didn't believe you about being broke."

"Well, I am. *We* are. We have just enough to get to Kantor's house. Enough for gas. You know my credit cards won't work."

She went on, "I think it's that big van and, of course, that hunk of diamond on your finger."

I looked down at my hand. "I had forgotten all about the diamond." I laughed. "Yes, I bet they thought we are just pulling a fast one on Rosa."

"You know, we—you, I mean—*could* hock that ring."

The ring, a champagne pink diamond, had been a gift from my deceased friend Clover. Ordinarily, I didn't wear it, but when we had left Fort Worth, I was sure not going to leave it for Mr. Hamra to find. It was worth over three hundred thousand dollars, but I never thought of it as valuable in that way. It was valuable to me because of Clover not as a meal ticket. Still, it could come to that. If we didn't find Bondesky.

"We have to find Bondesky," I told the bedraggled Janie.

"I need to shower."

"There's no water."

Eventually, Janie washed off at the beach, which was still closer to the bookstore than it used to be. There were also some strange new dunes near the property. Janie dried and dressed in clean shorts in the stuffy, hot apartment, shrieking every time she saw a crab scuttle across the floor. The small translucent crabs were everywhere. They were even coming out of the electric outlets near the baseboards.

I refused to check out the bookstore again, knowing I would be heartsick and full of guilt for leaving it in such a mess.

"I'm sticky, sandy, and hungry," Janie said as the van pulled out onto the sand-covered street.

"But lucky," I reminded her as we crossed the causeway in perfect weather. The van dripped mushy dog food as we looked out on the sun-bright bay.

"Did you remember to get Harry's piece of paper?"

"Yes, it's right here in my shorts."

"So now all we've got to do is find Bondesky."

"And Twenty Wigmore Street. Wherever that is."

"And someplace with a shower."

We rolled off the causeway like someone getting off a midway ride.

Janie didn't even look behind her at the shining sea. "For our next vacation, Honey, can we go to the mountains?"

"Gee, I don't know. Do they name avalanches?"

Eighteen

We had enough money for a cup of coffee and a slice of grapefruit pie at Savage's, the little fruit stand and gas station about an hour north of South Padre Island, where I filled up the gas tank, but that was it. "No more cash," I told Janie. "I'll have to borrow some money from Kantor until we get back to Fort Worth. We can't even afford *those* oranges now," I said as I indicated Savage's cart full of fake oranges. Presumably the real ones were inside.

"I am so sorry I don't have any money, Honey. I've been such a drain on you. I promise I'll get a job just as soon as we get back from London."

"We're not going to London. I'm going to exchange those English pounds for cash, but, just out of curiosity, where is it you are planning on working?"

She gave me a serious answer. "Waffle House, I think. I've been practicing saying 'Do you want cream with your coffee?' and I think I've got it down pat. And of course we have to go to London. Both of us. Four eyes work better than two. You can't get your money back for those tickets. And if what you said is true, Harry is somehow tied up with Steven Bondesky. And they are both missing and we have to find them. Not just for their sake, heaven knows, but for ours, too. No Bondesky, no money. No Harry, no peace of mind. And . . ."

Before she could go on with her *ands,* I stopped her. "I can't deal with that right now. First things first. First we find Kantor. You read the map to me. You know how lost I get when I'm not on a familiar route. I really need to concentrate on driving. I bet my car insurance has lapsed, too."

Janie rose to the occasion and six hours later navigated me through Austin's traffic to the turn-off to Fredericksburg, the one we had passed before in our pursuit by Sledge Hamra. Just reaching that point in the highway made both of us think of the man. "Wonder where he is now?" Janie said in an idle query.

I thought I knew where he *had been,* but I didn't have an answer for her now. Who *was* the man who died in the knee-high surf outside the bookstore? And was the man I saw attack him really Sledge Hamra or another bald-headed man? And had he actually killed the stranger in front of my eyes or had he been trying to help him? And, of course, there *had* been a gun. Maybe I should have said more to the Coast Guard about what I saw.

Nahhh.

My experience with police—and their military counterparts, I was sure, were of the same ilk—was that they only tied you up in red tape and never solved a thing. My prime example was my police friend, Lieutenant Silas Sampson of the Fort Worth Police Department. He meant well. I knew that. He was just so limited when it came to creative ideas pertaining to catching murderers. I really liked Silas—he was the first one to crack the shell of isolation I had lived in for years—and we had even had a flirty nonflirtatious relationship for a while. Now we were good friends and sometimes lunch buddies. I hadn't called him about Bondesky's disappearance, and I certainly wasn't going to tell him about something I *might* have seen in the middle of a hurricane. So there.

"Here," said Janie.

"What?"

"Here is where you turn off for Fredericksburg. Coming up, that is. Wouldn't it have been easier to do this from San Antonio?"

"I only know one way to go, and this is the way I usually go. And yes, now that you've asked, it *might* have been easier from San Antonio, but *we're* doing it from Austin."

I quit my musings and focused on the situation at hand. "Now we'll get some answers. That is, if Evelyn Potter really is with Kantor. Maybe we won't even have to worry about gas money home."

"Honey, I've been thinking. You know when those men at the bookstore—those Red Cross people, insurance people—whatever they were . . ."

"Yes, I know who you mean."

"Well, you know when they said that they were sending that dead man to Austin? For identification?"

"Yeah. What about it?"

"They were lying."

"I'm not following you. Lying about what?"

Janie turned in her seat to face me with a dead-serious look. "They don't do it that way. Small towns like South Padre Island or even Port Isabel don't have the lab facilities to do the fingerprint or dental detecting, you know?"

I nodded. "That makes sense. That's why they send the body to cities like Austin."

She lowered her voice to a whisper, "That's just it. They don't send the *body*. They send the fingers. Well, they send the whole hand."

"Get outta here," I screeched. "No way. You're making that up."

"Seriously. I went to this crime seminar. I told them I was writing a mystery, and they let me in, and they told us all kinds of interesting things. They cut the hand off at the wrist and put it in a bag and . . ."

"Stop it," I demanded. "That's enough. Next you'll be telling me that they cut the head off to get the dental records identified."

"Well . . ." she said.

"Don't even go there," I warned.

"Okay, but let's just say I don't think you should apply for a job in the mailroom of a big city crime lab."

I had to laugh at that despite the gory images her words conveyed. I tried to erase the conversation from my head, but one thought stuck. "Janie, I didn't know you wanted to write a mystery."

"Sure, someday. Hey, I figure I've read so many of them, I might as well write one. I do plots in my head all the time. Just never have had the nerve to sit down and put them on paper."

I shuddered as I thought of what she had told me about crime labs. "I bet you've come up with doozie plots."

"Not half as good as what we've been living

through lately. Our lives seem to be stranger than fiction. One adventure—murder—after another. Now we're off again. From one clue to another. I can't wait to hear what Evelyn and Kantor have to add to this new plot."

"We're not in the middle of a murder mystery again, Janie. This is real life, and there's bound to be a sensible explanation for all of it." Lord, I could hear my mother's voice echoing out of my head.

So could Janie. "Yes'm," she said with a crooked smile.

I pulled up at a four-way stop. "Now which way to Kantor's house?"

"You've been here before. I thought you knew."

"Once. I've been here once. Before he built the cabin. When it was just property and a dream. Outside Fredericksburg, that's all I know."

"According to the map, it's left. Make a left turn here."

"Making left turn," I announced. My spirits rose just thinking we might get answers soon.

"Honey, *your way*—the other left."

"Left. Right. What's a little turnaround among friends?" I was getting downright giddy with being so close to Evelyn Potter and the answers we needed.

Kantor's dream/retirement cabin was a few

miles down the road. A handmade sign announced our arrival: *Kantor's Kabin.*

"So he isn't original or even creative. Main thing is we found it and, Janie, we've found Evelyn, too. Look there."

Evelyn Potter's sensible gray Ford Escort was parked next to Kantor's maroon vintage sports car, and Evelyn herself was parked next to my old mentor Kantor on the front porch of the cabin that faced the small pond he called his lake. They were rocking side by side, drinking something that looked cool and inviting in glasses so cold I could see the frost on them from the road.

"We'll take two of those," I shouted to the couple as Janie and I got out of the van. I let Bailey out of the back, and he bounded away, happy to find dry ground and grass again.

"Are they alive?" asked Janie in a hissing whisper.

"What do you mean?" I turned from my protective watch over Bailey to look at the two on the porch. I could see what Janie meant. Steven Bondesky's secretary, Evelyn Potter, and my good friend Kantor were stone still, staring at us as if they had seen ghosts.

I waved to shake them out of their trance. "Hey, guys. What's going on?"

Nineteen

Despite their looking as if they had seen the dead come to life, both Kantor and Evelyn rushed down the deck's wooden steps to welcome us. That their effusive greetings didn't quite make up for the first awkward reaction to our appearance was lost in the social exchanges and exclamations over our hurricane story.

"We had no idea you two were on the island," said Evelyn. "I would have just died worrying about you." She put a delicate hand to her throat to show her concern.

Reassured that she did indeed care about my welfare, I decided her initial reaction had been to our finding her alone at the cabin with Kantor. She was probably just embarrassed to be caught in a compromising situation.

Kantor covered his composure by pulling on the ends of his plum satin vest and asking, "What in the Sam Hill is that on your van? Did you drive through wet concrete?"

"It's dog food," I laughed. "Dried dog food."

The little man herded us back to the deck as Janie and I told them about the garage and how Janie had swam in the dog mess and before I knew it, I found myself drinking a tall Tom Collins in my very own frosted glass, and Janie was off to the showers.

I tried to chat with Kantor, but he seemed so nervous to be with me that I was bamboozled. This was not the man I had known since I graduated from junior college and began working for Constant Books. This was not the man who had shown me how to mix the love of books with the life on the road. I couldn't believe that his fidgety posturing was because Janie and I had found Evelyn and him alone in the cabin. It was like he was hiding something from me and knew he wasn't very good at it. Like he was afraid he would spill the beans without Evelyn at his side; he kept glancing over his shoulder and calling out to her to join us, but she was busy with Janie.

"This weather is so unpredictable. That's what

Evelyn and I were doing out here on the deck. Trying to see if we could see the storms approaching. We're under a tornado alert, you know."

"Tornado alert?" I looked up at the blue sky.

"Yes, from the east. Remnants of Hurricane Charley. The storm traveled the same path you did from the valley. It was just off to the west. Now it's turning east, they say on the television. I don't know how safe you're going to be here, either."

So what was he saying? That he wanted me to go?

Janie came outside. She was wrapped in what I guessed was Kantor's striped terry bathrobe, her wet hair dripping on its collar. "Honey, you won't believe this. Evelyn says we're under a severe weather watch. There could be a tornado, even. What is it with us and weather?"

"Kantor was just telling me about it. I hate to admit this, but we forgot to listen to the radio again. Too lost in our thoughts, I guess." I got up to give Janie the bag I had retrieved from the van. "Just put on your bathing suit," I told her. "Looks like we're never going to reach dry land."

She went off to change, Evelyn clucking after her like a mother hen.

"Kantor," I said seriously, "I really need to talk to Evelyn."

"I'm sure she will join us in a minute." Reluctantly, he added, "Anything I can help you with?"

"I don't know. It's about Steven Bondesky. You know. My accountant? Of course, you do. Evelyn must have told you about him. Well, he's missing, and I need to find him. There's this problem with my money . . ." The words that bubbled out of my mouth seemed to make Kantor more nervous. I hushed my tirade about the money and said cautiously, "Maybe you can answer some questions for me? He disappeared with my money about the same time Evelyn came to work with you." I saw the same strange flicker of fear in his eyes that I had seen when we first arrived.

Maybe it was just the weather.

Kantor's salt-and-pepper mustache twitched on his face. In fact, I thought I saw his bow tie bobble above his white shirt collar, signaling deep distress. He suddenly jumped up from his deck chair next to mine and ran to the railing. "Honey, look there. Oh, I love this Hill Country. Can see forever. Wonder how far off that is? See how the blue meets the gray? Would you look at the size of that wall cloud? That's a classic weather front moving in. We'd better get an update on the television. I'll be right back." And if I thought Evelyn Potter had scurried off like a mother hen, I'd have to say Kantor was acting like a scared rabbit.

I jumped up and followed him into the rabbit

hole which, after a serious warning from the television weatherman, eventually led to an inner closet in Kantor's Kabin peopled by two weather-wearied women, Steven Bondesky's secretary Evelyn Potter, and a very nervous Labrador retriever. Kantor made it into the group just as the first hail hit the roof. He had scampered to the kitchen to rescue the gin and Tom Collins mix. He handed me an ice bucket as he closed the door to our improvised tornado shelter. Janie held the flashlight, and we all refurbished our drinks.

"Too bad I didn't snatch up the playing cards," Kantor joked as his knee hit my chin. I ducked from the blow and knocked heads with Janie. We all took a minute to get a feel of our own space. Elbows and hips vied for the most comfortable resting places in the cramped closet. Kantor sat squatted near the door, his knees drawn up under his chin. Evelyn's shapely form just seemed to mold against the back of the closet while Janie and I fought it out for any remaining space. Bailey lay half on my lap and half on Janie's. I rested my drink on his back.

Overhead, the storm gods played Star Wars with lightning rods and hail dice.

I had to shout to be heard. If I was going to die right here in the middle of Texas Hill Country, I by God was going to know the answers I wanted to hear. "Evelyn," I shouted. "Where is Bondesky?"

Evelyn must have thought she was going straight to hell if she didn't answer truthfully, and she screamed into the storm, " He's in Mexico."

Twenty

Huddled on the floor of Kantor's closet, Evelyn Potter finally lost all her mystique for me. She screamed as loudly as any of us did, and it wasn't just in response to my question about the whereabouts of Steven Bondesky. The fierce twister that took the roof off *Kantor's Kabin* also blew away the weather angel that had hovered over our heads in South Padre Island.

Janie had a death grip on my arm, and Bailey was buried under my legs. I don't know why they thought I was their anchor in the storm. Kantor was still standing, and Evelyn had both her arms thrown around his legs. I hadn't been so scared since I had found myself in a locked room with a roomful of armed women. Only this time I wasn't tied to my chair. There was no chair.

The tornado blew over in a New York minute, but it seemed that it lasted for a lifetime. The sky that we could now see over our heads grew lighter, and the rain slackened.

Kantor carefully opened the closet door. It was all that was left standing. Maybe the weather angel hadn't flown so far from us after all.

The tornado blew away most of Kantor's house, Evelyn's Ford Escort, and all the hopes I had for getting a further answer to my question. With rain pelting in our roofless closet, Evelyn gaped at me through wide eyes and finished answering my question, just as if we were still sipping drinks on the deck: "He's fine, Honey. Just fine." She didn't have a platinum hair out of place. I patted my frizz top, which had spun with the cyclone, and asked, "What hair spray do you use?"

That Kantor was also in a bit of a shock was not surprising. Ten minutes before the tornado hit, he had his dream house, his dream woman, and a long-wished-for book in production. Now all he had was a chilled pitcher of Tom Collins drink and three bedraggled women—well, *two* drenched women and one obviously covered with Teflon— and a dog. His lovely sports car was in the middle of his lake, which wasn't as deep as it appeared but was deep enough to hold the classic car.

"Good closet," Janie told Kantor as she patted him on the shoulder, edging her way out the door into a pile of rubble. "You know, that sounded more like an airplane landing than a freight train. Good lord, Kantor, would you look at this?"

I stepped over what used to be Kantor's bed frame and asked, "Evelyn, if Bondesky is alive and well and in Mexico, then where is my money?" I wasn't being insensitive to the situation; I happened to need answers, and I figured that my questions were going to get lost as soon as everyone came back to earth.

Evelyn actually snarled at me. "How can you think of money at a time like this? Kantor has just lost everything." That thought caused her arched, plucked eyebrows to swing in Kantor's direction as she reassessed his market value.

Bless his little heart, Kantor raised the drink pitcher in a salute and took a long drink from the glass he still held in his hand. "God bless the USA!" His bow tie bobbled as he gulped back tears.

I thought he had lost his marbles in the twister, but Janie grinned and said, "You lucky dog."

"Pardon? I don't understand," I said.

"Kantor is insured, Honey. And he had USA insurance with complete tornado coverage and he

will come out looking like a rose." Kantor tugged
at the ends of his satin vest and nodded assent.

"That's smelling like a rose," I countered as I
wondered how she had figured all that out from
his outburst. I guessed it was from all those years
of writing down shorthand notes in her omnipotent
clue notebook. And selfishly I yelled, "Where is
my money?" I kind of felt like Scarlett standing in
the turnip field.

Fortunately, everyone ignored my foot-stamping
and went about trying to collect bits and pieces of
Kantor's home. Evelyn was especially pleased to
find her Lancôme makeup bag. We loaded the van
with the remnants of Kantor's life as Janie and
Evelyn vied for giving directions on *what to do
now*.

What to do involved driving to downtown Fredericksburg, where we encountered people bent
over in the "tornado stoop," picking up pictures
and papers from sodden clumps of soaked gray
matter strewn around the streets. I stopped the van,
at Kantor's order, by a man standing in the middle
of the street wearing cutoffs and a tall Uncle Sam
hat. Instead of enlisting in the army—as I had first
thought—Kantor simply gave the man his name
and policy number. After a quick call on the USA
agent's cell phone, the agent wrote out a check
right then and there to cover Kantor's initial recovery payment.

"It's that easy? That's all there is to it? Why don't I have USA coverage? Oh, maybe I do. Bondesky would know." And I continued my ongoing glare at Evelyn Potter, who clutched Kantor's insurance check to her ample bosom. Other than repeating "He's fine," I hadn't gotten any more information out of her about the accountant's disappearance.

The Uncle Sam agent came over to the driver's side of the van. "You got USA coverage? Looks like your Plymouth Voyager has suffered some damage. You drive through wet cement or something? How about your house?"

"My house is fine, and that's dog food on the fenders. Unless you have a chisel, I don't think we'll be doing business here." I added, "How bad was the tornado? What are you hearing?"

"Actually, everyone is happy," Uncle Sam said as he removed his red and white striped hat to reveal a shiny bald head that reminded me of Sledge Hamra. "Just property damage. And it didn't cut a very large swath. No deaths like in Jarrell a few years ago." He wiped his head with a handkerchief and yelled toward the back of the van. "Now ya'll will be in Fort Worth, right? I can reach you at this number?"

Kantor grunted assent, and we drove off toward the interstate.

Taking Kantor and Evelyn home to my house had been Janie's idea. It would never have occurred to me to shelter the homeless there, but as soon as Janie learned that Evelyn had sublet her house for six months when she left Fort Worth to go work with Kantor, she was struck by a lightning thought. "This is providence. Kantor and Evelyn can stay at the house and keep Bailey while we're in London. I was afraid we were going to have to leave him with Sledge. I don't know why we couldn't take Bailey with us. After all, his owner is British. What a stupid quarantine law. Do you think if we went through France we could sneak him onto the ferry or maybe the Chunnel and get him to London? I know he's not a bloodhound, but I bet he could track Harry."

Janie's babbles evoked questions from Evelyn and Kantor. They were snuggled into the middle seat while Bailey was delegated to the back one. Evelyn sure had become fonder of Kantor again when she realized he was not only not going to be without money, but probably even a little better off after the final settlement from USA.

Kantor was quiet. In shock, I surmised. On the one hand, he was cool and debonair about his loss. On the other hand, he was devastated. He just stared at the passing scenery as Evelyn rearranged what was left of his life.

"Kantor can research his book at the TCU library, and I'll stay home and keep dear Bailey company. I think it is so wonderful that you and Janie are going to England, Honey. You must not be as desperate for money as you pretend. You girls! If you only knew what real poverty was. Ya'll just go on and have your English fling."

"We're not going to London," I muttered under my breath, but it sounded just like that: sputtered mutterings, signifying nothing.

Twenty-one

Everyone fell into an exhausted sleep except me, the driver.

I ran through options in my head as the van ate up the four hours of road between Austin and Fort Worth. I could cash in the English pounds and have a small reserve. I could go to London and find Harry. I could hire a real private investigator to find Steven Bondesky in Mexico. I could go to the police. I began the litany of choices for the tenth time when I heard Janie talking in her sleep.

"One hash brown. One grits. Waffle Plate over light, scrambled, hold the grits."

If Janie could dream about going to work, well, so could I. I remembered a training seminar I had attended at Constant Books. The counselor had taught that if you couldn't come up with a creative solution, to stand on your head. "Look at the problem upside down," she had instructed. "Forget traditional methods. Be creative with your problem solving."

Maybe it was time for me to learn acrobatics.

Traditional methods sure weren't getting me anywhere. Janie and I had concluded in a roadside rest stop that Evelyn was lying, lying, lying about knowing where Bondesky was. And that she had shared the information with Kantor and that neither one was going to spill the beans.

"It reassures me that Evelyn doesn't seem worried about Bondesky," I told Janie over the stainless steel stall. "That's a good point. Means he's not kidnapped or arrested or anything. Bad point is that I still don't have information about my money. Another good point is that I don't believe for a second that Kantor would keep something from me that would hurt me."

"You know, I think Evelyn really doesn't know about the money, but she did get twitchy when you asked her if she knew what Wigmore Street meant. I wish she wasn't so loyal to Bondesky. I thought when you quit working for someone, loyalty went out the window, but oh, no . . . not with our Evelyn. She absolutely refused to confirm whether Harry is Mr. Bondesky's client or not."

"Well, she is dead set on us going to London. Maybe that's a clue without telling it outright?" I stared at myself in the stainless steel mirror. "These rest stops are sure vandal proof. You can't even get a clear image in these fake mirrors. I know I can't look *that* bad!"

Janie raised her eyebrows. "You haven't had a shower since Padre. Or changed your clothes. You've been though a hurricane and a tornado in those shorts. I'd say the mirror is pretty accurate."

We got back in the van, and my four passengers dropped off to sleep, leaving me with the road and my thoughts.

I had it all worked out by the time we reached Washington Avenue.

Janie ushered Evelyn and Kantor into the house while I walked around back with Bailey. The dog's needs always come first.

First thing I noticed was Sledge Hamra's black truck parked in the clinic parking lot that adjoined my property. It looked shiny and clean, but when I walked over and ran a finger under the front bumper, loose sand fell into my hands and onto the asphalt. The kind of sand you find at a beach. "Aha, Bailey," I said in my Sherlockian voice. "Our PI has been on a vacation, too. He was at Padre. I didn't imagine it all." I looked up at the architecturally starved third floor of my house. "I have a few questions for you, my friend," I shouted to the vacant windows.

Janie came running out the back door. "Honey, we've been robbed."

My first thought was that we had nothing to be robbed of, then I realized there is more in the world than money to steal. "Oh, lord, I knew I shouldn't have left that man here. What's missing?"

"Strange things. I mean we've been robbed and not robbed. Exactly. He left notes."

I followed Janie into the kitchen. There was a gap on the cabinet where my new microwave had stood. A grubby Post-it note declared that the microwave was "on loan" while our heroic PI financed his newest lead. He had taken the microwave as well as my big-screen TV, my new Dell computer, and my new dishwasher.

"Nothing seems to be missing of your mother's, Honey."

"I'm not surprised. I told Sledge I would kill him if he touched one thing that had belonged to my mother."

"Where do you think he's gone? The notes say he will pay you back for it all. Should we call Silas? Oh, dear, I just don't know what to do."

"I do."

"You're so calm. I thought you'd die when you

found out you were right about Sledge Hamra and I was wrong." Janie's cornflower-blue eyes filled with tears.

I always do best with a plan. My mother had taught me that. It wasn't my natural inclination to think ahead, but her years of training hadn't been in vain. "Get me my Day-Timer," I bossed. "I'm making out a list."

Two hours later, I was down to the last item on my inspired list.

First had been a bath.

Second was to throw away the clothes I felt had become a part of me and as hard to remove as dried dog food from a fender.

Third was a call to Constant Books.

The fourth I implemented when I dialed Minnie Hudson.

Minnie was the friend I should have had growing up, but I got Steven Hyatt instead. I loved Steven Hyatt, but the giggling and head-knocking girl talk Minnie and I had enjoyed at The Bargello during the summer had reminded me that my childhood had been less than classic. Minnie was my age and weighed about a hundred pounds more than I did. Her mother dragged her to the spa whenever she could, although losing weight for Minnie would cause a drastic career change. Tall and beautiful beyond words, Minnie was a successful plus-size model who laughed and toned during her weeks at The Bargello with her mother. "I love Ma, but, good honk, I wish she would accept me as I am."

We had first met under false pretenses; she had thought I was Janie's daughter and very, very rich. (Well, I had been then.) That she hadn't turned her back on me after the truth came out gave her a permanent top-of-the-list mark in my book.

We had kept in touch and had promised to meet again. I knew where to find her.

She was living in New York, working on a spring catalogue.

I tracked her down at the studio.

"Honey Huckleberry? Is this really you? How in the hell are you?"

I ran through my mental catalogue of recent complaints and decided the weather bulletins and robbery, not to mention the loss of my money, could wait. I got right to the point. "Minnie, are you up for a trip to London?"

"You're heading across the pond, are you? I love London. Yes, yes. Count me in. When do we leave?"

Evelyn brought me in a grilled cheese sandwich and iced tea. As she sat it down by the telephone, she whispered, "Ask her if she knows Wigmore Street."

Stunned though I was by Evelyn allowing a disloyal clue pass her lips, I did just that. After all, it was the next thing on my list.

"Wigmore Street? Near Selfridges? I know exactly where it is, Honeychile. Near Saint Christopher's Square where they have this darling little Italian restaurant that serves the world's best teramisu. Why? What's on Wigmore Street?"

I looked down at the two brass keys I had put on a special key ring. One was to Harry's Sandscript Bookstore in South Padre Island. I just knew the other would fit a lock at 20 Wigmore Street. I just *knew* it, but I told Minnie, "A hunch. It came to me when I was standing on my head."

Twenty-two

As Minnie put words into action, I remembered another reason why I wanted my money back.

Money talks.

And what it said to Minnie was that she could take my two tickets to London and upgrade them to first class so that they would be next to hers. "You sure didn't think I was going to park this classy ass down in a tourist seat for ten hours, did you?"

Janie was relieved that she was still included in the expedition. "You ever heard of the Three Musketeers, Janie?" I had asked her. "Well, that's us. You, Minnie, and me. You surely didn't think I would leave you alone at home when there is real detecting work to be done. Why, I wouldn't know anything at all about mysteries and murders if it wasn't for you." Before either of us could figure out if that was a positive conclusion, we were packed and on our way to London.

I had thought to reassure and entertain Janie on her first airplane flight as Steven Hyatt had done for me. It turned out that I wasn't over my flying jitters as much as I had thought, and it was Janie who wound up holding my hand and forcing Bloody Marys down my throat while the plane bounced over the remnants of Hurricane Charley as it continued to spread out toward the east.

She chattered incessantly, but that was nothing new. "Did you see that woman with the babies? I just know she's leaving her husband and going home to Mama. And did you notice that one man with the little boy? He's a divorced father and only gets the boy during the summer. I think they're heading for the Riviera. I hope he doesn't leave that boy alone while he gambles. I'm sure he has a gambling problem. That older couple behind us? You didn't notice them? I don't see how you could have missed them. I bet they're on their second honeymoon, returning to France where they went on their first honeymoon. And . . ."

"How do you know all this stuff? You're making it all up."

"I am not. I'm just a good guesser. And you

know how everyone looks like someone you know? I mean, that woman in the third aisle over looks just like Arthur Wescott's Aunt Selena. The spitting image. And I'm sure I saw Betty Turner from West back there near the toilet. I bet she is dying for a cigarette."

I fell asleep on my postage-size pillow while Janie rattled on about how much Betty Turner smoked. I went out so hard I didn't even see the Statue of Liberty when we arrived in New York. Janie punched me in the ribs with her elbow to wake me up to see it, but I missed it. We landed in New York in silence as the awesome sight of the statue stunned Janie to dumbness. I wished there had been a replica of it at the D/FW Airport.

She stayed quiet until we spotted Minnie by our London check-in counter. "Minnie, I saw the Statue of Liberty. I never thought I'd ever live to see the Statue of Liberty. I've got to come and see it in person. I mean not from the air, you know? And, oh, the things to see in New York. Times Square. I want to see Times Square. You must make me a list of things to see when we come to Steven Hyatt's premier."

"Janie, you ol' scoundrel you, give me a hug. I declare, I still think of you as Honey's ma. Been up to finding any killers lately? If you two don't beat the band, I'll eat my hat. And speaking of hats, I gotta say that's a mighty stylish one you're wearing." Minnie crushed us both in bear hugs. Her saucer-sized brown eyes were full of excitement, and there was no denying the delight she felt at seeing us. I let go of my guilt over asking her along.

Janie touched the brim of her tan straw hat. "You like it? Oh, good. I worried."

"That I wouldn't like your hat?"

"Well, with you being a model and all . . ."

"It's perfect. That red rose makes it."

"Oh, good. Yours and Honey's are in my sack here. Honey wouldn't wear hers."

"I can't imagine why, Janie. Give me mine. Look, perfect fit. Honey, I insist. You put yours on, too."

Minnie clamped the straw hat on my head, and we all stood there like three members of the Clampett family just in from the hills. Arriving passengers made wide detours around us, snickering behind their hands.

"I will not wear this hat," I hissed.

"Better than an umbrella like the tour guides use," Janie declared. "We'll never get lost from each other."

"That's the point," I said. "We're supposed to be anonymous while we're looking for Harry. Not like a hillbilly band marching down the middle of the street."

"Oh, ho. So there *is* a purpose for our trip to London?" Minnie cocked the brim of her hat and looked like she was ready for a fashion shoot. Janie just looked like Janie in a hat. As for me, I never wanted to see a mirror again if I was doomed to wear the group badge for the whole trip. Instead of the Three Musketeers, we looked like Larry, Curly, and Moe.

I took off the hat and pointed Janie toward the rest rooms. "Hurry," I told her. "We start boarding in just a few minutes." I confided in Minnie, " She wouldn't go on the flight from Dallas. She thought they would dump the toilets out like they used to do in trains, and she didn't want to ruin someone's picnic."

Minnie was almost bent over double from laughing. "I'd forgotten what a hoot you two are. Are you sure you're not really mother and daughter? And what's this about finding Harry? Isn't he that guy that lives on South Padre Island? Why do you think he's in London? And why are we searching for him? You're not pregnant, are you? Bet Steven Hyatt won't like that."

I sighed and began the tale that I thought she wouldn't buy if I had told it to her on the phone. I was as chatty as Janie as I related the events of the past week. The story took us onto the plane, into our seats, and way out onto the Atlantic before I drew a breath.

Minnie hung on every word, and we neither one paid much attention when Janie tried to tell us she swore she had seen her tenth grade biology teacher sitting next to Sledge Hamra back a tourist class. Having heard about my erstwhile private eye, Minnie wanted to go take a peek, but I continued on with my story, waving aside Janie's declaration with "Oh, guess my microwave didn't cover a first-class ticket. Reckon I should go back there and remind him that he didn't get my laptop computer? It might have made the difference in the cost of his ticket. Now, where was I in my story?"

Minnie worried, "Don't you think we ought to check?"

I smiled my Janie-wise smile, "Trust me, it's not him."

Twenty-three

"Okay, so tell me more about your Harry. If we're going to try to find him, I have to know more about him other than he has red hair and owns a bookstore."

Minnie and I were nestled down in our big beige leather seats, head to head, rehashing the particulars of the story I had told her. Janie was happily ensconced in a similar seat across the aisle with headsets donned. Every scene of the current Julia Roberts movie was reflected in her face as she listened to the sound track of the movie showing on the screen in front of her. It was a good time to confess to the secret I had withheld from Janie.

"Minnie, before I tell you about Harry, I want

you to know that this expedition is not just a lark. It's deadly serious."

"How deadly?"

"The real dead kind. You remember I told you about our rescue during the hurricane?"

"Yeah."

"Right before the Coast Guard drove up to the bookstore, there were two men outside. One of them had a gun and was trying to break into the store."

"Oh, lord. And what was the other man doing?"

"They weren't together. This one man had just broken the window over the door with his gun, and this other guy came out of the shadows—it was dark during the hurricane—and they started fighting. I'm positive it was that man I told you about, Sledge Hamra."

"The one Janie swears is a tourist?"

"Oh, don't pay any attention to that. I'm sure Sledge is on his way to Mexico to find Steven Bondesky. All he cares about is his money and his next meal. Janie has been seeing people she knows ever since we hit the D/FW airport. No, Sledge followed us to Padre because he thought we knew where Bondesky was hiding."

"Okay, go on. What happened to the man breaking into the bookstore?"

"This big man, the one I think was Sledge, came

up, and they started fighting, like I said. Then Sledge took this guy's gun and hit him on the head with it. He went down in the water. It was about knee high. And before anything else could happen, we saw the red lights on the Coast Guard truck. When I looked again, there was no one there. No Sledge. No stranger. But the Coast Guard did find a dead man near the bookstore."

"The same man?"

I thought before I answered. "I think so. It was hard to tell with all the rain and wind. They asked us to identify the body, but of course, we couldn't."

"You'd never seen him before?"

"Nope, but he was foreign looking. At first I thought he was Hispanic, but I decided later that it was more of an Arabic look. Like the guys who run the 7-Eleven near my house. They're from Pakistan. He was wearing a white shirt and black pants—no identification. The authorities in Padre told me they would let me know if they identified him. They had to send his body to Austin."

Minnie's wide eyes grew until they were pools of brown. "Do you know what they actually send to the crime labs? I read that . . ."

"No, no." I stopped her. "Janie has already told me, and I think you are both wrong." We sat in silence broken only by Janie's laughter as she enjoyed the comedy she was watching.

We both made a groaning sound as our imagi-
nations carried us into a crime lab investigation.
We laughed, and Minnie said, "Time for a subject
change. Tell about Harry."

"Hmm, how do I describe Harry? I've told you
what he looks like. And he's older than I am."

"No, you didn't mention that. How much
older?"

"About ten years, I think. And he is from England. You knew that. And he comes from a
wealthy family. He didn't ever say so, but when
he would talk about his past, it was always about
posh stuff. Not bragging, mind you, but more like
this was just his way of life."

"Why on earth was he at the ends of the earth
on South Padre Island then?"

"He said it was because he wanted to get away
from it all. Minnie, I didn't ask many questions.
That was before Janie dragged me into the inquis-
itive way of life. I just drifted through life, you
know. I liked him. We had this—well, this affair
thingie—and that's about all I knew. Oh, and he
has this limp. Not a bad one. From an injury when
he was in the Royal Navy. That's why he retired
early."

"Still, to come to the States and South Padre
Island. That's about as far away as you can get
from civilization and still be in it. You say he was

on good relations with his family, so it couldn't be them."

"I'm not following you," I confessed.

"Honey, it's perfectly clear. Harry was running from something or hiding from someone. Think about it."

I thought about it.

I thought about it through the rest of the flight. Thought about it until the flight attendants woke us up with warm wet towels to refresh us. Thought about it through the landing at Gatwick. Thought about it as I slapped the straw hat on my head as we deplaned.

Looking alike was not such a bad idea after all, I concluded as we wound our way among throngs of people into the holding area of the Gatwick Airport. After walking down a final ramp, we entered a cavernous room that would have held three of the jumbo jets we had just flown in on. At the end of the room, an array of customs desks forced passengers to form lines for entry into the U.K. Janie wound up in another line, but I could find her by the red rose on her hat, and she kept waving our way to let Minnie and me know she had us in sight, too.

I clutched my passport in my hand, ready to verify that I was indeed who it said I was. I don't know why it is that people feel so guilty when faced with official inquisition. "Just imagine, Minnie, this is how it must have been at Ellis Island for the immigrants."

Minnie looked around at the shoving strangers who all had business to get on with in London. "I don't think so," she said. "These people all look too affluent to me. You know what's wrong with air travel nowadays? When I first started coming to Europe with my folks, we all dressed up for the flight. Now you find people in their bathrobes making the trip. I'm a great believer in comfort, but air travel sure has taken a low-profile road."

"We're no prime example for the fashion industry ourselves." I smoothed the wrinkles out of my denim dress and straightened the collar on my maroon jacket. "If they are letting people in based on clothes, we'd all wind up being deported."

"Speak for yourself," she grinned. "They love leather here."

We inched forward in line, and I bumped into Minnie's back, the fringe on her brown leather vest caught me in the eye, causing tears to blur my vision. I looked like I was crying when it was our turn to approach the official. He was so bored with his job that I don't think he would have cared if I was bleeding from the nose.

"Pleasure or business?" the customs officer asked when it was our turn at his desk.

"Business," we both replied.

"Welcome to the United Kingdom, ladies." And he gave us a stamp of entrance on our passports.

"Now to find our luggage."

"That's it? We're in?"

"Yep, we just get our bags and go through that line that says Nothing to Declare."

"What if I was smuggling something? How would they know?"

"That's what I like about you, Honey, always thinking of the devious angle. Believe me, these guys are trained. You just look like a lost tourist to them. They hope you'll spend a great deal of money while you're here and perpetuate the legend of the kingdom."

"But what if I really did have something illegal on me?"

"Well, if they suspected it, they would pull you aside and do a search. You don't have anything dangerous with you, do you?"

"Just Janie."

"You told that officer that you were here on business. I didn't know you called hunting for a missing fiancé business." Minnie laughed as we made our way to the luggage carousel.

"It's not," I replied. "But the work I'm doing for Constant Books over here is. Reckon I forgot to mention it. I called them because I remembered that before I gave up my route, I had seen a flyer asking if there were any book reps traveling to England this summer. Constant has just taken on a new line called Dragon Flight, a sci-fi/fantasy publishing house based in London. I'm representing Constant in welcoming them to the fold."

"Won't that cut into your sleuthing time?"

"Nahh, all I have to do is meet with these guys at a book fair and say, 'Welcome to Constant Books.' It's more of a PR kind of thing. And I'm getting paid. Not much, but it beats 'one hash brown, scattered and smothered.' Look, there's Janie. She made it through customs, too. Guess the British don't think she looks dangerous."

"Who's that with her?"

With her red rose a bobbing, Janie greeted us in triumph at the carousel. "Honey, Minnie, I want you to meet Matthew Haney. Mr. Haney was my tenth grade biology teacher in high school. You remember I told you I saw him back there in tourist class sitting right next to Sledge Hamra!"

Minnie and I surprised the gentleman from Texas by swiveling our heads as if we were possessed by demons as we searched the Gatwick Airport for the elusive Sledge. "That big man that was next to me? Oh, he's already gone. Pushed by everyone and was the first out the door. I'm sorry you missed him. Is he a good friend?"

"Good question," I answered.

Twenty-four

Well, wouldn't you know it? One minute I'm standing at the train track outside Gatwick Airport, waiting for the express to London, and the next minute I'm kidnapped.

I had bent over to pick up the damn hat that had fallen out of my carry-on bag, and when I stood up, two men had me by the arms, guiding me away from the train platform and into an old blue car.

"Am I being deported? I swear I'm here on business, but pleasure, too. I could have said pleasure. Do I have to have a green card to work?"

All I got for an answer was a rude shove into the back of the car. As it sped away, I looked back to see Minnie and Janie laughing together as the train for London arrived. They didn't even know

I wasn't with them. I raised my hand to signal them, but the man beside me pulled it down and twisted it to hold me in the seat.

I was so scared I thought my nose *was* going to bleed. "What? What? What?" I kept asking. The whole thing was very disorienting. The man I thought was the driver turned around in the front seat. God, I thought, we're going to be hit by another car. Then I realized the driver was in the other seat. Right-seat drivers, wrong-way traffic. I tried to get a grip. "Who are you? You're not official, are you? I don't have any money, honest. It's all in Mexico with Bondesky." I was cursing myself for not having put the English pounds in traveler's checks as Minnie had warned me to do. At the time it had seemed like a lark to be carrying around foreign money. Oh, lord, if they searched me, they would find the fanny pack full of pounds under my dress.

I was trying to decide if I should just give them the money before they strip-searched me, when the guy in the front seat said, "We don't want your money." He spoke in a low voice, in an accent I didn't recognize.

"I don't have anything else. I'm just a tourist, see? Oh, lord love a duck, what on earth do you want?"

"Harry Armstead. We want Harry Armstead.

Now, little Miss Tourist, tell us where he is."

The man beside me bent forward and hissed in a garlicky breath, "Yes, tell us now or we will kill you." The wicked switchblade he pulled from the pocket of his black jacket would certainly be able to do just that.

"Harry? This is about Harry? How did you know I know Harry? And if you know that, you know I don't know where he is, either. Who are you? You don't look British to me, and why do you want to find Harry?"

"Slow down," the front seat passenger said.

"I'm talking as slow as I can," I responded. "Harry? This is about Harry?" I drawled out my words, trying to speak slower, but I realized as I repeated the questions that the man was talking to the driver. The car slowed to a normal speed and all three men looked out the windows to see if anyone was following or had noticed anything unusual.

The thug in the front seat grunted, "That is better, Masud. We don't want to be caught for speeding."

Oh, no, I thought. *Not when kidnapping and murder are such better charges.*

I was afraid but curious, too. Who in the world would know that I knew Harry? I looked just like any other tourist from America to me. Well, maybe the hat was a little much. "Where are you taking me?"

The driver spoke for the first time, "For the last ride of your life, if you don't tell us where to find Harry Armstead."

It was getting stuffy in the car. All three men smelled like old food and unwashed bodies. "Can you roll down the window a bit?" I asked.

"Harry Armstead," the man beside me demanded.

"Do you work at my 7-Eleven? Is that where you know me from?"

The long blade of the knife grazed my cheek. If it drew blood, I was too numb to notice, but I got the point.

"Okay. Okay. No reason to get so excited. I don't know where Harry is. That's why I'm here in London. To find him. We are in London, aren't we? I have his dog and I have the key to his bookstore, but I don't have Harry. That's why you look familiar. You're the one who got killed during the hurricane. Oh, I don't mean *you*, I mean someone who looks like you. Do you know Sledge Hamra? Is he the one who set you on me?"

This time I felt the blade of the knife on my cheek. "I didn't kill your friend, honest. Sledge did." I didn't feel the least bit guilty squealing on Mr. Hamra. If I was going to be killed, it wasn't going to be for a murder I didn't commit.

The car lurched to a stop.

The driver turned around slowly and faced me. He was a thin-faced, dark-skinned man with a mop of black hair that fell into his face. Even through the mane that covered his heavy lidded eyes, I could see the serious intent of his words. "The man who was killed in Texas was nothing to me. A hired hand, that is all. He was worthless. Harry Armstead killed my brother, and it has taken years to find him. Like the coward he is, he hid away from us, but we found him in the United States, and we will find him again. I *will* have revenge for my brother's blood."

"You must be mistaken. Harry wouldn't kill anyone. He likes books. And he has a dog. He has me."

"And you are going to take us to him, are you not?" He reached one hand toward me and stroked the cheek that had received the knife cut. Blood covered his finger as he pointed it at me. "We are going to watch you very carefully, you with the sweet name. And when you find Harry Armstead, so will I. And if you go to the authorities, I will know it. And if you make one mistake, I will know it. You will be very lucky to make it back to the States alive." He continued to caress my cheek. "Ah, but we do not want you. We want Harry

Armstead, but if we do not find him soon, I will take great pleasure in killing someone he cares about."

And he hit me.

I've never been hit before. Ever. And it hurt.

He hit me in the face. I fell backward into the seat. Involuntary tears sprang to my eyes. Before I could gather my bearings, the man beside me got out of the car and dragged me into the street. He handed me my purse and my carry-on bag, then slammed the straw hat on my head. He, too, reached out and touched my bloody cheek. Slowly he raised his finger to his lips and licked it. Then he smiled and got back in the car. It drove away at a legal pace, leaving me standing on a curbside in London.

"There she is. I told you she would find a way here. Honey, you missed the train ride to Victoria Station. I loved all those little houses we passed. Every single one of them had a rose garden. I'm going to love London. Minnie was worried about you, but I knew you would be okay."

I turned around to see Janie and Minnie standing beside a black London cab. The sign above the door of the building we were by read The Selfridges Hotel. I started toward them in a daze.

"Honey? Honey?" Janie was almost hysterical. "Your nose is bleeding."

Twenty-five

The fuss that they made.

No, I didn't need a doctor. No, I didn't need the police. I especially didn't need the police.

I told a lie to the worried concierge; some friends had picked me up at the airport as a surprise, and we had had a small collision on the way into London. I had hit my nose on the back of the front seat. That was all.

We were a pretty ragged bunch to be checking into The Selfridges Hotel. Talk about your low-profile tourist!

Minnie led the parade to our room as Janie and I tiptoed past tea tables and vases of flowers taller than any of us. She distributed pound notes to everyone she met and ensured that the occupants

of suite 537 were going to have privacy and ex-
traordinary service from the staff. I knew I had
wanted her on this trip for some reason.

As the hotel room door closed on the last of the
bellmen—we had more bellmen than bags—Minnie turned to me and said, "Now what in the Sam
Hill is going on? Who hit you, and who do I have
to kill?"

"You'll have to stand in line, Minnie," countered a snarling Janie.

"Has the bleeding stopped?" I took the wet cloth
the concierge had given me away from my face.
"And does anyone have a Tylenol? I have this
headache."

Both of my friends gasped, and Janie welled up
in tears. "Your face! You're going to have a black
eye. I *am* going to call the hotel doctor; I don't
care what you say."

I put my hand over hers as she picked up a
telephone. "Don't," I pleaded. "Just get me some
Tylenol, please. Is there anything to drink? Get me
something to drink, and I'll tell you what happened and why we can't call anyone."

Minnie took the phone away from Janie and dialed room service. Janie rummaged through her
purse and came up with a pain reliever. She also
found the small refrigerator and announced, "It's
fully stocked. There's orange juice and some red
stuff and some beer.

"Forget the orange juice," said Minnie. "I've ordered a couple of pots of tea and coffee, but until then, this is what she needs." And she whipped out a silver flask of what turned out to be scotch. It went down as smooth as silk.

Minnie took a drink herself and passed the flask to Janie, who also downed a slug.

They clucked like mother hens until I took a quick shower and got into bed. When the tea tray arrived, we all three sat cross-legged on my bed, drinking and eating wee sandwiches like we had never eaten before.

"Finger sandwiches," declared Janie. "Thank God they sent so many of them. I've never eaten a real cucumber sandwich before. Not bad."

Minnie scoffed two down at a time and said, "In England, it's *not half bad*. Means *good*."

Janie picked up on the saying quickly, "Well, these cream cheese sandwiches aren't half bad, either."

When we got down to the grapes and sinful slices of chocolate *gâteau*—which turned out to be chocolate cake—Minnie finally demanded answers to my distressed state.

I hesitated.

"Oh, no you don't!" she roared. "This is where it all hits the fan, remember? You can tell us the truth. We're the good guys. The ones in the white hats. Well, maybe tan hats, but just the same, Honey Huckleberry, Janie and I deserve to know and want to know what's going on!"

The scotch, the Tylenol, and jet lag all chimed in together in my head and told me I just wanted to sleep, but Minnie was right. If I was in danger, so were Janie and she. "There were these guys . . ." I began.

When I finished, they sat in a stupefied silence.

Janie finally said, "I've never known anyone who was kidnapped before."

"Well," I assured her, "it's a little different experience than eating your first cucumber sandwich."

"They're watching you? They're watching us?" Minnie got up and did a long-legged walk to the windows and pulled aside the drapes. "I don't see a soul who matches the description of those men, Honey. No, wait there's a man in black pants and a white shirt on a bicycle. There's another one walking a dog. Shit, they could be anyone." She turned back to face the bed. "The driver said Harry killed his brother? Your Harry is a murderer?"

"Now wait. The Harry I know couldn't have killed anyone."

"It's the Harry you don't know who worries me," she said.

"Well, you two worry me. I *have* to find Harry.

I have to warn him about the kidnappers, but you and Janie aren't involved in this. I thought it would be fun—the three of us coming to London. And I thought Minnie could help us cut through the getting lost bit, but now I see that ya'll are in as much danger as I am. Soon as I get a little sleep, I'm going to come up with a plan, but I can tell you already it involves you two going back to the States ASAP."

They ignored me with exasperated sighs and long glares.

Minnie said, "Let's sleep on it. You're right about one thing. We are all suffering from jet lag. I'm beginning to see double. We've been up almost twenty-four hours now."

"Is that what it is? I thought my eyesight was going. I'm off to bed. The door is locked, isn't it?" And Janie fell into the bed next to mine.

Minnie stopped at the doorway leading to her room and ran her fingers through her chestnut hair. "You sure as hell better love this guy, Honey, or you're going through a lot of grief for nothing."

I fell into such a deep sleep it was like being hypnotized. I was asleep and could hear my own exhausted breathing, but on the other hand, I was awake and staring at the ceiling. People walked in and looked at me. One reached over and touched my eyeball. In my dream, I called out for them to stop it. A dream Bondesky came in and said, "Well, you really done it this time, Huckleberry."

The waking dream deepened when Silas Sampson appeared and whipped out his notebook. "How many kidnappers were there, Honey?" Janie was behind him with her notebook; she asked, "And which one were you going to marry? The one in the front seat or the one in the back—the one with the switchblade?"

My father came and took me by the hand. "Come, my Honey. There is a way out. Don't be afraid." And he handed me a telephone without any cord. My mother answered the call and said, "I told you not to slide down the banister, Honey."

Someone walked in and touched my eyeball, and it started all over again.

Twenty-six

I woke up with the bedside telephone in my hand.

So, with the help of the hotel operator, I called Evelyn Potter back in the States.

When I told her about the kidnappers, she pawned the phone off to Kantor, who didn't have a clue as to what to say. "Bailey is fine," he reassured me. Well, of course Bailey was fine. It was *me* they were after, I thought.

"Put that coward Evelyn back on the phone," I demanded. "Please," I added. Whoa, I was getting pushy as I got older. "Evelyn, this is it. The sticking point. I don't care if you pledged allegiance to the President of the United States; I want to know what is going on. And I know you know something you're not telling. Why is Bondesky in Mexico? And why won't you admit Harry is Bondesky's client? What's all the mystery here?"

"Honey, really, I didn't know it was going to be dangerous. I would have told you before this. I thought it was some lover's game. Mr. Armstead leaving you the clues and all."

"Clues to what?"

"When he was here in the spring he, Mr. Armstead, that is, met Mr. Bondesky and hired him. Oh, Mr. Bondesky said it wasn't in his usual realm, but for you, he'd do anything. That was before he got sick."

"Harry's sick?"

"No, no. Mr. Bondesky is. Oh, I don't think they call nervous breakdowns sick anymore, do they? He was disturbed. Yes, *disturbed* over Clover Medlock's death. He couldn't get over it. Like he could have prevented it or something. He really loved her, you know. He had all his life. That's why he never married anyone else."

"He told you this?"

"Yes, when I found him crying in his office one day. Right after the funeral. He couldn't stop crying."

"Why didn't you call me?"

"Oh, he was adamant about that. He didn't want you to know he was what he called 'weak.' We worked it all out. We found this clinic in Mexico, a very good clinic, where he could go and rest for awhile. He's a lot better."

I remembered my hasty phone call from Bondesky while I was searching his office. "He sounded okay to me, a little disoriented; he didn't know who he had called, but okay. All right, I'll buy that. I'm sorry I didn't know about his breakdown, though. But where does Harry fit in all this?"

"For some reason, Mr. Armstead was apprehensive about his future. He wanted to make sure you were safe. I thought he meant financially, but I can see now I was wrong. He was afraid to leave you anything directly, so he had Mr. Bondesky set up this system."

"System?"

"Yes, if anything happened to Mr. Armstead, you would both be notified, and when you asked Mr. Bondesky about it—he said you always came to him for advice—he would give you a key. It's one he has in a special file at the office."

"I have the key," I told her. "Keys," I corrected.

Evelyn didn't ask how I got the key from the orange file in Bondesky's office. I don't even think she heard me. She was far too intent on telling me now what she should have a week ago. "The key is to Mr. Armstead's flat in London. He left it to you. Like in a will. And Bailey. He wanted you to have Bailey."

"Is his flat on Wigmore Street?"

"Yes, that's the one. Did you say you have the key?"

"Yes," I replied absently. "Evelyn, does any of this have anything to do with my money?"

"Oh, no. I don't know anything about your money. Before he left for Mexico, Mr. Bondesky had some kind of security system put on his computer. All the financial records are in there. But, don't worry, Honey, I'm sure Mr. Bondesky arranged to keep your money safe. He loves you like a daughter, you know."

"Does loving me like a daughter include hiring a private eye named Sledge Hamra? Maybe to be a bodyguard or something?"

"Oh, no," she said again. "I never heard of Mr. Hamra before you mentioned him. But I know one thing; he is not a client of Mr. Bondesky. And Kantor and I have been keeping an eye out. We haven't seen hide nor hair of him."

"Well, he doesn't have any hair, and I have seen him. That is, Janie has. Here in London. You don't need to worry about him anymore."

"Honey? Honey, are you there?"

It's a bad habit of mine to stop and think while I am on the phone. "Yes, Evelyn. I appreciate the information. If you talk to Bondesky, give him my love. No, wait, that would be too much for him. Tell him I said to ask the old bastard when he was going to give me my money. He'll understand that more."

"That sounds harsh, Honey. He's been a very ill man."

"Nahh, it's what he would expect from me. That's the kind of father/daughter relationship we have. If I sent him my love, he would think he was dying."

"Speaking of dying . . . well, I hate to say this, but if you have the key to the Wigmore Street flat, does that mean that Mr. Armstead is dead?"

"Not yet," I told her. "And not if I can help it."

I hung up the phone, breaking the connection to the States.

No wonder I couldn't figure any of this out. Too many secrets. What a world this would be if everyone and their dog didn't have secrets.

If Harry had told me he was hiding from someone or even if he mentioned that he had killed someone, I wouldn't be in the spot I was in. And Evelyn: If she had told me about Bondesky's breakdown or if he had . . .

Did I have any secrets?

Oops, yes, I did.

I reached across the foot of floor that separated

Janie's bed from mine and shook her. "Janie, wake up. I want to tell you about this dead man in Padre. And while I'm at it, do you have any secrets you're hiding from me?"

Janie rolled over with a pillow-creased face and mumbled, "Secrets?" She held up a mashed mess of unidentifiable material. "I thought everyone saw me take this last cucumber sandwich."

Twenty-seven

It was a beautiful plan. A one-of-a-kind plan. A foolproof plan.

"It ain't gonna work," Minnie said.

Janie was more diplomatic. "Why don't we just wait till night and disappear into the fog? No one can follow us through London fog."

"Did you ever hear of the Clean Air Act?" I asked her. "There is no more London fog except on the label of American-made coats. You and Minnie said you were not leaving and that you wanted to help. Well, this is your chance."

We were standing by the hotel entrance with a group of students and teachers, waiting for the tour bus to pick us up for a day trip to Stratford. There were so many passengers that half were standing in the street. A big green bus with a Stratford Tour sign turned the corner.

"This is it," I declared. "Now, do your stuff."

Janie took the straw hats from Minnie and me and started circulating in the crowd, her mouth going as fast as it could. In just a few seconds, she had several women raise their hands. She chose a slender woman with short red hair and gave her a hat. Then she smiled and handed one to a taller woman. When the bus pulled alongside the crowd, all three of them climbed the steps, chatting and laughing.

I pulled the dark blue scarf over my head and looked around. "I know if anyone is watching now they are watching those hats," I whispered to Minnie, who was hunkered down to a mere five foot four.

"Fifty pounds apiece for a bogus public relations campaign is a bit steep I think," said Minnie.

"We had to be sure they would wear the hats. That was the deal, twenty-five pounds up front and twenty-five more when they reached Stratford. I figure if anyone is following the bus, they will figure it out by the time everyone gets off, but that will give us enough time to do some unrestricted snooping. Do you see anyone?"

"Yes, two cars. There. They just came out of nowhere, but they are following the bus. I think."

I could barely contain my excitement. "That's them. That's them. In the blue car. Masud and the boys. Oh, wait. In the gray car? That's Sledge Hamra. Oh, dear, what if I've made a mistake? What if Janie is in danger?"

"I have a feeling that when the Arabic men meet Mr. Hamra, Janie Bridges will be the last person on their mind. Relax, it worked. Look."

The two cars were following patiently behind the tour bus as it turned onto the next street.

I still had my doubts. "I don't know. I don't think it was such a good plan after all. I kind of forgot that where there was a boarding, there had to be a deboarding. Maybe we should find a taxi and go after them."

"That street the bus turned on? That's Wigmore Street. We're that close. Janie is having a lark, trust me. Besides, she gets to be a tourist for a day. You know she'll love that."

Reluctantly, I nodded my head and glanced around me for any stray, remaining watchers. The coast looked clear to me. We quietly left the safe shadows of the hotel marquee and started strolling down the street toward Wigmore.

At any other time of my life, being in London, walking down a London street would have been one of the highlights of my life. My family had come from England, albeit Liverpool, and I had always wanted to visit. Sneaking down the street while looking over my shoulder hadn't been on my wish list of things to do in London.

"Now, act casual, Honey. Just walk on down the street. We'll walk on this side by the IBM building then cross over and go back right by Number Twenty. That's it there, Number Twenty. The one with the glass door and the brass handrails up the stairs."

I looked across the narrow street and wondered, not for the first time in my life, how remarkable it was that given a number and a map, you could find anything anywhere. You just kept heading toward a destination and finally, there it was, right where it was supposed to be. Number Twenty had started out as part of an inked note taped on the bottom of a dog food bowl and, lo and behold, here was the real thing.

Number Twenty Wigmore Street appeared to be a very respectable yellow brick building with a few people coming or going through the glass and brass door. Ordinary looking. A dentist proclaimed on a small discreet sign that he had an office on the ground floor. A barrister announced his presence with a similar brass sign.

We walked by once on the Number Twenty side of the street. At the corner by the post office, we turned and retraced our steps. The third time by

the door convinced us that if we didn't do something, it was going to make for a boring adventure.

"Let's stop here for some coffee and see if anyone is following us," suggested Minnie.

The Breakfast Scene was a small café two buildings down from Harry's. We had toasted breakfast
tea cakes and coffee as we sat facing the window,
carefully scrutinizing each passerby. "They all
look like normal people to me. Well, the ladies in
the saris would be kind of out of place in Sundance
Square, but maybe not. The world is getting so
mixed up nowadays. Seems half the world is moving to Fort Worth sometimes."

"Good economy, cheap flights," said Minnie.
"Want some more coffee? I'll buy us another cup.
They don't know the meaning of the bottomless
coffee cup over here. Every cup is a new adventure." She got up to go to the counter. "More tea
cakes?"

"Just coffee, please."

We drank the coffee, and it was my turn to buy.
"How does my eye look?"

"Not bad, considering. The scarf helps. Does it
hurt? And the knife cuts are already healing. You
won't have scars. You want some Advil or something?"

"Not really. I'm fine. Really."

We sat there for a while longer. A long while.

"You know, if we're going to get something done before those goons get back from Stratford, we'd better get on the ball."

I said, "Yeah, I know. It's just kind of scary, you know? I don't know what we'll find when we get there."

Minnie looked out the window for the hundredth time. "I swear I don't see a soul who looks dangerous. Want to try to get in the building?"

"Why not? It's not like I don't have a key."

Twenty-eight

Armed with courage and sloshing with coffee, we finally entered the doors at Twenty Wigmore Street. The small foyer led off to hallways that included the dentist's and barrister's offices that we had seen advertised in front. A small dark counter at the rear of the foyer signaled a registration desk and attendant.

"I don't know the room number," I whispered to Minnie.

She smirked and said, "Watch this." She took an envelope out of her model's bag and folded it in half. She wrote Harry's name on it and took it over to the desk. "I need to leave a note for Mr. Armstead. Will you see that he gets it?" And she included a five-pound note with the envelope.

The appreciative clerk took the envelope and turned immediately to squirrel it away in a pigeonhole behind the desk. "Done," he said.

"Thanks awfully much," Minnie replied with one of her best catalogue-shot smiles. She walked back to me and made like she was rummaging in her purse. It was large enough to hold half of Texas, and it could take hours to rifle through in a serious search. "Is he looking?"

"He did for a minute. Now he's doing some papers. Turning around. He's turning around."

"Good. Make a dash for the stairs."

We slipped out of sight of the clerk and through the door marked Stairs before he could complete his turn to the front again. As far as he knew, we had gone through the front door to the street.

I was impressed and told Minnie so. "That was a cool trick. Do that often?"

She smiled a self-satisfied answer and said, "Flat number three-oh-five. Means it's on the fourth floor."

"Don't you mean the third floor?"

"No. The fourth floor. Here they call the first floor the ground floor and the second the first and so on."

There was no one on the fourth floor when we cautiously entered the hall from the stairs. Flat number 305 was the second door on the right.

We took a deep breath, and I inserted the key I had ready in my hand. Before I could turn it in the lock, it swung open.

"Uh-oh," I said. "This doesn't look good."

We tiptoed into the apartment, and I called out in a loud whisper, "Harry? Harry? Come out, come out, wherever you are?"

"I think someone's been eating my porridge," said Minnie.

"What? Oh, yes. Someone's been here."

"Well, go on. Look around."

"I'm afraid of what I'll find," I confessed.

"Pooh. I've lived in New York. Seen one ransacked apartment, you've seen them all. Honestly, Honey, there's no one here. Shit, would you look at this mess? Or is Harry the normally messy type?" She gingerly toed scattered clothing away with her shoe as she entered the living room.

I followed behind. I had found one dead body in a living room in my lifetime and wasn't anxious to encounter a second. "No. I mean he's not a neatnik, but this is definitely vandalism. Nothing under those clothes, is there?"

"Just more clothes. I'll check the bedroom." She disappeared down a hall and shouted back to me, "Make that bedrooms, plural. Hey, I like this flat. Two bedrooms, kitchen, bath. Old Harry has pretty good taste. Wonder what a place like this would set you back?"

I was busy going through some papers I found on the floor by the dining room table. "Well, we can pretty much guess who did this."

"Your kidnappers."

"Yes, or Sledge. We can't forget Sledge. I just can't figure out where he fits into this picture."

"Find anything interesting?"

"How would I know? I don't know what was here, so I don't know what's missing. I recognize some of Harry's shirts, so this really is his apartment. Or he was using it. And some of these photographs I recognize. This one is his mother. Oh, and this frame held one of Bailey and me. It's gone. Ripped out. Some of it is sticking in the frame."

Minnie was in the kitchen. "Want some coffee? There's a Mr. Coffee here."

"I don't think I could ever drink another cup again. Which reminds me. Where is the bathroom?"

"I'm going to make some anyway. It's off the end bedroom. I think that must have been Harry's. There're more clothes strewn around back there. You know, Honey, if Harry left you this flat, it means we're in your place, right?"

I left her question unanswered as I found the bathroom. I didn't want to face the fact that if this was my apartment, it meant that Harry was dead.

I washed my hands and looked around the wrecked bathroom. I picked up an aspirin bottle and put it in the medicine cabinet. As I closed the door to the cabinet, I saw the note taped to the mirror.

Minnie came down the hall. "There's even a washer and dryer. Actually it's a combo thing. First it washes, then it drys. What's the matter? You look like you've seen a ghost."

I handed her the note I'd taken from the mirror.

"Oh my: *'First the girl then your mother give yourself up.'* Pretty much to the point, isn't it?"

"I think I'll have some coffee," I said.

We took the note and the coffee into the living room where Minnie cleared a pile of junk off the couch. "Okay, we'll just sit down and try to make some sense of all this. *'First the girl.'* That's got to be you, right? *'Then your mother.'* That's Harry's mother, I bet." She looked up from the note. "Honey, what do you know about Harry's mother?"

"Nothing, really. I mean he *has* a mother. He called her Mother. I reckon she would be Mrs. Armstead. That's it. He never talked about her other than sometimes to say my mother this or my mother that. You know. Just conversation things. His father's dead, I do know that. And he is an only child."

"This part of the note that says, *'Give yourself*

up.' I'm guessing that the note is a threat. Like give yourself up or we will kill the girl, then your mother. Wonder if Harry has seen this note? I mean, you can leave all the notes in the world, but if someone doesn't read it, it's like whistling in the wind. Harry may not know you're in danger. Or his mother."

"There's no way of telling; but, Minnie, something has bothered me. If Harry intended me to have the apartment—the flat—if something happened to him, why would I get the key in the mail if he were okay?

"Honey, face it. This story may not have a happy ending. Harry may not be okay."

"No, I don't buy that. If Harry were dead, then I wouldn't have been kidnapped yesterday. If they'd found Harry, they wouldn't need to intimidate me. No, he's out there somewhere; we've just got to find him."

"Okay, I'll go along with that. Where do we start looking?"

I picked up the frame from the table and looked at the picture of the woman it held. "With Mother, of course!"

Twenty-nine

There was a listing for a "Mother" Armstead or rather an Eleanor Armstead in the phone guide, but no address, and no one answered the ring. The other Armsteads we did contact never heard of our Harry. Instead of being stumped, Minnie brilliantly put in a call to a private taxi company. "I've driven with Edmund before. He was the driver on a shoot we did in Dover once. He's an actor, drives when he's not auditioning. He knows everyone. If anyone can find our Eleanor, Edmund can."

She arranged for Edmund to pick us up at The Selfridges Hotel, which gave us a chance to change into some higher-class sleuth clothes; however, it didn't matter what I wore, Minnie always outshone me. I watched as she swept her hair into a fashionable twist on top of her head, held in place with silver clips. "You look like you could go on a corgi run with the Queen," I told her. "And I look like I could clean out their cages."

"Pooh, you look great. Here, let me just fix that collar, and I'll just loan you this pin for your jacket. There, see? I'll run with the dogs, and you have high tea with Her Majesty."

Despite the fact that our mission was so serious, we were, after all, young and in London. We kept our good spirits as the darkly handsome Edmund drove us to Harry's mother's house. That the driver knew exactly where we wanted to go did not surprise Minnie, but I was in awe. "Millions of people here in London, and you know one address?"

"Right on, luv. Bred and born here, I was. Know these streets like the back of my hand. Yes, know the streets, know the houses, and know the way to the kitchen doors for a cuppa and a squeeze, if you get my drift."

"And you know Eleanor Armstead?"

"Oh, right. She and her mister used to do a lot of entertaining. Keeps a great cupboard, or did. Haven't heard all that much about her since he died. There's a son, too. Or did he die?"

That put a damper on my good humor, which finding myself parked in front of an immense stone house surrounded by a high wall and black wrought iron fence did nothing to quell. "Harry lived here? Grew up here? I never knew. He never said."

"You think this is grand, eh? Well, lass, you should see their country home. Drove some parties out there for a weekend several times. Now, it's what I call posh."

"And what do you call this? Never mind. Oh, Minnie, I don't know if I can do this."

She bustled me out of Edmund's cab. "Of course, you can. Remember, it's a matter of life and death."

I was mumbling about living on the south side of Fort Worth and not knowing anything about grand houses and weekend parties when Minnie pulled the bell chime that hung by the front door. "Oh, can't you do it gentler? That's so loud."

"Not loud enough to get anyone to answer, though, is it?" And she gave another tug on the rope. "This is a little much, I agree. A simple buzzer would work, in my opinion."

"No one's coming. Wonder if there's a servant entrance? There's bound to be. I can't see the upstairs maid using the front door."

We found another door, smaller and less intimidating, around the side of the house. There was still no answer, and we peeked in the bay windows near a little herb garden to no avail. "Face it, Minnie. There's not a soul here. Should we wait awhile?"

Edmund joined us in the kitchen garden. "Chap next door, the butler actually, says the house has been closed for a couple of months. Mrs. Armstead is ill, he says. She's in a sanitarium south of London. Haywood Heath—small town."

"Sanitarium? She's crazy?"

"No, Honey, here a sanitarium is like a nursing home back in the states. People go there to recover. Of course, she could be crazy, too."

"Want me to pop you around there, then?"

"How far is it? We don't want to miss Janie at the hotel."

Minnie looked at her watch. "Her tour is due back in London around five-thirty. It's only after one now. I think we can make it there and back with no problems. What do you think, Edmund?"

"No problem. Traffic is light today. Not as many tourists this time of year, and it's not a weekend. If we're off right now, we can motor there and back in two hours. That gives you plenty of time to talk to Mrs. Armstead. If she'll talk, that is. I was right about the son. Fellow says he died, and that's why the miss's is in the sanitarium."

Edmund's statement hit me like a stake in my heart. "He says Harry died? Oh, no, I don't believe that for a minute. Let's go. If Janie gets back before we do, she'll just have to manage." I led the way to the cab. I didn't need to look back to know that Minnie and Edmund were shaking their heads and rolling their eyes.

Harry is not dead. These words in my head became my mantra for the drive to Haywood Heath. They carried me through the cheese and bread sandwiches Edmund picked up for us at a pub before we left London. I don't even remember eating mine, but a faint taste of sawdust in my mouth assured me that I had. I drank my bottled water and watched suburban London through unseeing eyes. As long as I kept saying *Harry is not dead,* he wouldn't be.

The sisters at the sanitarium assured us that Mrs. Armstead was feeling better today, and that they just knew she would enjoy seeing the daughters of her friends from the States. "So this is like a religious place?" I asked Minnie as we followed a starched uniform down a hallway.

"No, they call all nurses in England sister. Oh, maybe it does go back to religious times. Funny how things stick. I can tell you one thing, what this place is . . . is expensive."

Eleanor Armstead wasn't in her room—a light and airy place with flowers and linen curtains blowing in the breeze from an open balcony—but after a hurried consultation with a lesser sister, she was located in a garden nearby in a gazebo surrounded by wheelchair-sized paths and wood ferns. We found her stretched out on a white wicker chaise reading a book. Her white hair—dressed in a casual knot—still bore a trace of Harry's auburn color. When she looked up, it was like looking into Harry's blue eyes.

I nodded to Minnie. It was the right woman.

"Mrs. Armstead?"

"Yes? The sister said you're daughters of friends of mine? I don't believe I know you, though." Mrs. Armstead smiled a gentle smile and seemed relaxed and open to our confrontation. Not like someone who was recovering from the loss of her only son.

But as soon as I said, "Actually, I'm a friend of your son, Harry," she closed the door to her face. Tense lines formed around her eyes, tearing away at the carefully tended face. Her complexion went from a healthy glow to ashen parchment. We watched as Eleanor Armstead aged twenty years right before our eyes.

Tears spilled over the pale blue eyes and ran down the new wrinkles on her cheeks. "Harry? Harry's dead."

Thirty

We arrived back at the hotel just after Janie did. We found her munching more cucumber sandwiches from a fresh tray and enjoying a pot of hot tea.

"You really like those sandwiches, don't you?" asked Minnie as she snatched one up on her way to the bathroom.

"I do. I do. May I pour you a cup? I'll be the mama. I learned today that the one who pours is always *the mama*. I think I can even get the mixture right."

"What else did you learn today?" Minnie handed me a cold, wet towel, which I draped over my sore and tired face.

"Poor Honey," Janie commiserated. "Here,

here's your cup. I could hardly enjoy the tour, knowing you were so banged up." She raised the towel to look at my face. "Hmm, your eyes are both swollen, but only one is black. The knife scratches are doing okay. Are you using the Neosporin like I told you to? Have you been crying? What's happened?"

I took a sip of the hot tea and said, "Give me a minute, and I'll fill you in. What about you? Did the kidnappers follow you around Stratford? And did you know that Sledge Hamra was following you also?"

"Your Masud and his men took off toward London the second they saw that it wasn't you and Minnie wearing the hats. I hope that gave you two enough time. What was at Wigmore Street?" She didn't wait for an answer but went right on, "And, no, I never saw Sledge Hamra, but then I didn't know he was following me, too. I guess I let my guard down after the kidnappers drove off. We went to Shakespeare's home and the Gildhall. My favorite stop was Anne Hathaway's cottage. Now I know what they mean by an English garden. I've never seen the likes. And . . . let me see . . . oh, yes, we stopped by Warwick Castle on the way back to London. It's modernized. You know— they have a bathroom right where an old guardhouse stood. They even have peacocks on the lawn, and one came right up to the window in the rest room and yelled at me." She finally ran down. "Oh, but I guess you don't want to hear a tour guide version, do you? Bottom line, the blue car left as soon as we reached Shakespeare's house, and I never saw Sledge."

Suddenly, Janie looked concerned. "I'm not a very good sleuth, am I? I got caught up in the tour and all."

Minnie fetched me another cup of the reviving tea, and I roused to tell Janie that she had done a splendid job. "We would never have been able to cover as much ground as we did if you hadn't tricked our followers out of London. I feel like we've been through a forty-eight-hour day."

"Tell," she demanded.

Minnie and I both began to relate the day's events to Janie, starting with the tea cakes at The Breakfast Scene, when we were interrupted by a knock on the door. Minnie cautiously opened it and admitted our driver Edmund. After introductions to Janie, he said, "I went right back to the Armstead house, like you said, and talked to that chap next door again. He said Harry Armstead died in the States about two months ago."

"That's not possible," I declared.

"Well, now, that's what he said."

"Oh, Edmund, I'm not doubting your report, but

if Harry died in the United States, then why did I find his stuff, things I know he had in Padre, at Wigmore Street?"

Janie choked on her sandwich. "Harry's dead?"

So we told her the story of the afternoon—how we had gone from Wigmore Street to Haywood Heath, how Harry's mother Eleanor had broken down when we mentioned Harry's name, and how we had called one of the sisters for aid.

"They took her back to her room, and we never got a chance to ask her anything else," Minnie said as she picked up the story. "The sisters made us leave, and so that's why we sent Edmund back to the Armstead house to find out more information. That's all you learned, Edmund? That Harry supposedly died in the U.S.?"

"No, he said we weren't the first to come looking for your Harry. From the description, I'd say it was your kidnappers who were looking for him, too, but that was weeks ago."

"Honey refuses to believe that Harry is dead," Minnie told Janie.

"Well, me either," she said.

"Because . . . ?"

"Think logically, Minnie. Its what they do in the books. Look at the facts. If Harry was really dead and, let's say the kidnappers killed him, why, they would be the first to know. Right? And so they would have no reason to take Honey yesterday."

"That's what I've been saying," I agreed. "Janie, you're a wonder. Now, see, I told you I needed you on this trip. I just wasn't standing on my head to figure it out. Minnie, you've got to agree. Harry's *not* dead, after all."

Minnie still disagreed. "I don't know. His mother convinced me. I've been around a lot of actresses, and I don't think you could fake that kind of grief."

Edmund chimed in, "And that bloke next door was dead cert that Harry is dead."

"Let me think. Let me think," I implored them. "There's an answer in here somewhere."

"Are you going to stand on your head?" asked Edmund, who obviously took my earlier statement literally.

"Order a another pot of tea, and I'll show you," I laughed.

"Better yet, Edmund. You go around to the liquor store and get some Bell's and I'm ordering something from room service more substantial than these finger sandwiches," ordered Minnie. "A little scotch and a few hamburgers, and we'll have a real think fest here."

It was hours later when we came up with our new plan. Janie was asleep on the couch, and Edmund was about out of it, too. Minnie and I were invigorated with our current idea and still churning out scenarios. She told Edmund, "You go on home now and come back about ten tomorrow morning. We'll all be fresh then, and we need you to help us in case the kidnappers become violent."

The driver looked startled when Minnie mentioned violence but agreed to return the next day to help work the plan. I think he would have followed Minnie through fire, but he said as he left, "You could just go to the coppers, you know."

"We could, you know," Minnie said. "Edmund may be right."

"How do the British say it? Sorted out? No, Minnie, it's not all sorted out yet, but I promise you, if this doesn't work, I'll be the first in line at Scotland Yard tomorrow."

Thirty-one

My assignment was the Golden Triangle, the area that tourists visit most in London. My route began at Trafalgar Square right at Lord Nelson's stone feet.

Janie's was touring the same area in a double-decker red London bus, and Minnie got the tube route.

"I'll take the high road and you take the low road," Janie sang to us as Edmund put her on the correct bus that would take her around the triangle.

Minnie shouted after her, "Well, if you get to Scotland before me, order me a whiskey." She headed off in the direction of our Oxford underground station. "Actually I like the tubes," she said as she waved good-bye. "They're what the New

York subways *should* be. I've just never spent the day doing nothing but riding them, though."

Edmund was to be the semibodyguard and runner between the three of us. We had hired him for the day. He drove me to Trafalgar Square and wished me luck.

In our straw hats with the bobbing roses, we were sitting ducks for whoever would be watching us. Which was the plan.

"Now, whoever is approached by Masud first is to tell him that Harry is dead. And that he can leave us alone. That his vengeance is served, or whatever," I had instructed the three.

"You're sure they're still watching you?"

"Oh, yes, Minnie. Masud was not one to give up. Remember, he said he had been after Harry for years. He'll quit when he finds that Harry is no longer with us. Of course, not that I believe he's dead. That's immaterial. The one we have to convince is Masud."

"Well, he won't be looking for me," declared Edmund.

"Don't be so sure. If he saw you with us yesterday, he might just want to question you. I read somewhere that Arabs like dealing with men much more than women." I couldn't tell if that fact quelled his enthusiasm or not, but nonetheless, we all headed off in our appointed directions by ten-thirty.

I chose the National Gallery as my first stop, followed by the National Portrait Gallery. Someday, I thought as I strolled through the galleries, I would like to come back and really see what I'm seeing instead of having to concentrate on who's *not* seeing the paintings with me. I just knew I was being followed.

By the time I reached Saint Martin-in-the-Fields tearoom I *knew* it. I took a cup of tea from the attendant and forgot once again to say, "Black, please," and wound up with another cup of white tea. I can't stand milk in tea. I took the offending cup to a table near the Brass-Rubbing Centre, wishing I had time to make a rubbing of Lady Margaret Peyton, circa 1484. Lady Margaret seemed to be the most popular of the brass plates, and I watched three sets of tourists make rubbings from the replica of her tomb plate.

"Bet I wouldn't tear mine," I said aloud as I watched another disappointed visitor leave with a ripped souvenir. "Bet it's all in the wrist."

I was writing down, "Come back and rub Lady Margaret," when Edmund hissed at me from the shadows of the dark church basement. "Honey, no one has seen Masud. I've checked in with Janie and Minnie. Any luck on your end?"

"No," I said into the dark corner where he stood. "But I've got this feeling . . . well, I can't explain

it. We're close, I know it. Well, I'm off to . . .
to . . ."

"Saint James Park, down The Mall."

"Right." Edmund knew my schedule better than
I did.

By the time I had walked from Saint Martin's
to Buckingham Palace, I was exhausted. I had
barely glanced at the Clarence House where the
Queen Mum lived, and could have cared less that
it wasn't time for the changing of the guard at
Buckingham. I made my way down to Westmin-
ster Abbey, waving halfheartedly to a beaming
Janie who passed by on her bus; she must have
made The Triangle route about sixty times already.
She shook her head vigorously, signifying that she
hadn't seen a soul as her bus rumbled on down
the street. But she still looked spry and rested, I
thought resentfully. I tried to remember why I had
assigned the walking part of this plan to myself.

When I reached the abbey, I sank down in a
folding chair near the high altar. Several robe-clad
monks were doing what appeared to be a dress
rehearsal of some kind. One of them reverently
carried a sword on a pillow. I heard one of them
say, "Now imagine that the queen is seated here."

I looked at the seat next to mine that he indicated. The only person sitting there was Edmund.
"This is an honor," he said like the tour guide he

really was. "That's the Seed Pearl Sword carried by the Lord Mayor of London. They must be getting ready to have a dedication of some sort."

"Well, they'll have to have it without me," I said. "I'm dead. I feel like jumping up and saying, 'Ollie, ollie, oxen free' to Masud or whoever it is that I think is following me. Or shouting from the altar, 'Harry's dead, come out, come out, wherever you are.' "

"I'd say you're getting punchy," he said.

"Let's just say if the queen really were sitting here, I wouldn't have the strength to give her a nod. No one ever told me that being a tourist was so exhausting."

"I just came to tell you that our Minnie is about to give it up, too. I think she's lost her love for the underground. She says to tell you she'll meet you in half an hour at the Lord Wellington Pub. It's on the first street to your right when you leave the abbey. They have tables outside. We'll wait for you there." He left the queen's pretend chair and disappeared.

The chase was off. The plan hadn't worked. So be it.

I relaxed and decided to at least do one enjoyable thing before I met them. I headed for the Poet's Corner and lost myself in the midst of the memorials and tombs of the great writers. I passed

Geoffrey Chaucer's tomb and laughed when I remembered that Ben Jonson's epitaph, "O rare Ben Jonson," also meant in Latin "Pray for Ben Jonson."

It was dark and quiet in the Poet's Corner. Late afternoon, and not a tour group in sight. I turned finally to go and meet Minnie and Edmund, wondering how we could signal Janie to debus, when I bumped into someone—someone I knew: Mr. Sledge Hamra himself.

"About time," I said.

He was still wearing his American-sloppy clothes, and his head was shining with sweat. "I need to talk to you," he said hastily. "You've got to stop . . ."

Whatever it was I had to stop, I didn't find out.

One minute he was speaking to me and the next, gone. *Poof.* Just like that, as what was probably the final tour group of the day poured into the Poet's Corner. They swirled around me, causing me to step on Mr. Jonson's plaque. "Excuse me," I said to the dead writer and hurried back to the door of the abbey.

Outside, I forgot which was right and which was left. Did Edmund mean for me to turn right as I came out of the abbey or as I was entering it? I chose the wrong way, of course, and it was almost an hour later and many, many blocks before I found the Lord Wellington Pub.

Minnie and Edmund were sitting impatiently at a street-side table. A waiter was bringing them fresh drinks and took my order for a glass of bar scotch. "With ice," I shouted after him.

I told them about seeing Sledge and that I was more frustrated than ever.

"You had more success than I did," said Minnie. "I rode from Oxford to Marylebone and back to Waterloo and then to Ravenscourt. I went all the way out to Shepherd's Bush, for God's sake. I never want to hear another violin or flute echoing up those tube escalators again. I used to think the sound was so romantic and haunting. Ha! Drink up. You're way behind us."

"You didn't see anyone?"

"Not a soul. Oh, well, that is, I did see scores of Arabs. I told each one of them that 'Harry is dead, leave us alone.' It's a wonder they didn't call a bobby on me. And we have another problem."

In response to my questioning look, Edmund said, "We can't get Janie off the bus. She just keeps going round and round. She's getting more agitated. I expect her to jump any minute now. Look, here she comes again."

And sure enough, the red double-decker bus lumbered by us, a frantic Janie waving from the topside. Edmund stepped out onto the curb and

made a pulling motion with his hand like he was
switching on and off a cord. "Third time I've done
that," he said. "I feel like a fool. All she has to do
is go down the steps and pull the cord. Oh, look
the bus is stopping. By George, I think she's got
it." Edmund did a quick tap dance on the sidewalk,
which reminded me to tell Minnie for Edmund not
to give up his day job.

We sipped our drinks as we watched Janie run
pell-mell up the street.

"What do you think Sledge meant when he said
you've got to stop?" asked Minnie. She waved en-
couragingly to a flagging Janie.

Edmund held up his glass of dark ale to hurry
her on.

"I don't know. I haven't the faintest idea.
Maybe he was trying to tell me that Harry really
is dead and I should stop all the looking. And, in
fact, I'm sure he's right. We gave the kidnappers
every chance in the world to molest us again, and
they were a no show. I'm afraid I'll have to face
the truth. Harry's dead, and that's that. Otherwise,
Masud would surely have taken the bait."

Janie arrived at the table and breathlessly tried
to talk, but nothing came out but gasps. She
reached rudely over the table and grabbed up Edmund's ale, which she drank greedily, spilling
drops of the beer down her chin. "I saw him," she

finally managed to get out, sputtering beer in all our faces.

"Sledge Hamra? I know. I saw him, too."

"No," she continued to gasp. "Harry. I saw Harry."

Thirty-two

A twilight rainstorm impeded our progress to the site where Janie swore she had seen Harry Armstead from her bus-top vantage. Edmund carried one umbrella, and he kept trying to share his "brollie" with all three of us, a knightly gesture that left us all drenched by the time we reached the pub that Janie had seen Harry enter.

She had told us it was the Ruffled Peacock or the Purple Pheasant. "It had something to do with birds. Oh, I was trying so hard to remember the name," she wailed.

It was Edmund to the rescue again, faring better than he had with his umbrella: He finally exclaimed, "I know, the Royal Raven."

"Yes. Yes, that's it. The Royal Raven. Told you

it had something to do with birds. Now I don't remember which street though."

"I do. I know it. It's not that far, and it'll be quicker to walk than for me to go get the car. Follow me." And he led us on a fast track down side streets that ultimately led to the Royal Raven, which we discovered to be down by the Thames. It was a long walk and made me wonder just where Edmund had parked his car.

The street was dark, not only from the billowing clouds overhead and the descent of the evening, but also because the small, narrow lane was hidden among tall, surrounding buildings; it was almost an alleyway between major thoroughfares. One murky orb light weakly illuminated the weathered Royal Raven sign that swung from rusty iron rings attached to the light post.

"Certainly has lots of aromatic atmosphere," Janie said.

"It downright stinks," countered Minnie.

"What would Harry be doing in a place like this?" I wondered as I looked around. "What were you doing down here, Janie?"

"I couldn't help where the bus went, now could I?"

We were all panting from the fast pace and long distance we had covered and not a little scared and irritable. "Well, you didn't say you crossed any bridges."

"You'd be surprised what I crossed today, bridges being the least of it. Well, are we going in? It's been over an hour since I saw Harry go in, and he might be gone by now."

Minnie was still suspicious, "You're sure it was Harry?"

"As sure as I am that it was Sledge Hamra sitting back in coach on the plane," said Janie, reminding us that sometimes she *could* be right.

"I'll go first," Edmund volunteered.

"Now what good would that do?" asked Janie. "You don't even know what he looks like." And with a deep breath, she pulled open the dark door and entered the pub.

"In for a penny, in for a pound," Minnie quoted as she followed her into the Royal Raven.

That left Edmund and me still dripping on the stoop outside the pub. "Well?" he asked.

"I'm going. I'm going. I'm just suddenly overcome by maybe seeing Harry."

Janie reopened the door and pulled me bodily inside by the tail of my drenched sweater. "We don't see him anywhere. You look."

The four of us huddled in a wet mass by the door. It was darker inside than out; dim lights hung high near the ceiling, lit by what had to be forty-watt bulbs. "Wait, I have to adjust my eyes. I mean, they have to get used to the light. Ah, there *are* people here."

The few pubs I had visited with Minnie and even the Lord Wellington where we had met today were my ideas of what a pub should be. Dark paneling and tables with benches for people to relax and enjoy a pint of ale. Dartboards had been prevalent and the whole atmosphere was like being in someone's club room. The Royal Raven was a little different: Peeling paint of an indecipherable color hung from the ceiling and walls. There was an odor of dirty bodies, curry, and stale smoke. Groups of men huddled around small, black tables, and it seemed they were all staring right at us.

Minnie peered into the room. "None of them at the tables look like Harry. In fact, all of them look like your description of the kidnappers. That's it. I'm outta here."

I stalled her with my hand. "That's because you're not looking in the right place. There, behind the bar, that's Harry."

"I was right," Janie squealed.

"Hush. Everyone is looking at us. I don't know if these guys are the kidnappers or not, but if they're not, they're their cousins. Minnie, you and Edmund stroll over to the bar. Janie and I will follow, and I'll do the talking. Okay?"

Who was going to argue with the only one who had a plan?

"We'll have three whiskeys and a Guinness," I

told the bartender, who just happened to be Harry Armstead. He wore dark pants and a wrinkled white shirt rolled up at the sleeves. He was dressed like most of the pub's patrons who, in fact, were all men.

"Right," he said and began to fill the order. He gave us our drinks, and we drank them in silence, staring intently at a Harry who acted as if he didn't know any of us. That he hadn't had an affair with one of us for almost two years. Like we were complete strangers.

"Harry, it's me," I whispered as he fussed about, giving me change from my twenty pound note. I added, "Honey," in case he had forgotten my name, too, but I couldn't catch his eye. Then, "Huckleberry," in case he thought I was just flirting.

"You must be tourists," he said in a bland voice. "The change is enough. Tourists always overtip." And he pushed the remaining pounds into my hand. "Is that it, then? Or do you need another round?"

I was too astonished to answer, but Janie came to the rescue. "That's it; you've got us pegged. Lost tourists, all right. This is quite enough, thank you. I've just remembered the way home. Well, the way back to the hotel. We've got to run now, leaving in the morning. Back to the States and all. Well, thank you, and good-bye."

Before I could utter another word, I found myself back out on the rainy street. "What on earth,
Janie? That was Harry, and you know it."

The door to the Royal Raven opened, and one
of Masud's cousins came out. He stood on the
stoop and stared at us, which made me reconsider
lingering in the area. "Right, then, we're off," said
Edmund as he guided me away by the elbow.

Minnie looked back down the street as we
rounded the corner. "He's still there. No, he's going back in. He's gone."

I pushed Janie's hands away from my sweater.
"Quit dragging me. What was that all about? You
know that was Harry," I said again.

"Sometimes I wonder about you, Honey Huckleberry. You've got to quit reading romances and
concentrate on mysteries. That was Harry, yes, and
it was a Harry trying not to bring attention to you.
Or to him. I'll have to think about that. Which one
of you or us was in danger?"

"Janie, I'll show you some danger," I threat-
ened. I knew in my heart that Harry knew me and
that it was some kind of perilous game he had been
playing in the bar. I was embarrassed and ashamed
of the amateurish way I had acted in the pub, and
yet I still childishly was taking it out on Janie. I
knew I hadn't played my role well in the Royal
Raven.

Edmund restrained my arm with the purse I was getting ready to swing at Janie. "Hang on, luv, she's right."

"You could feel it," agreed Minnie. "Smell it, even."

"What? What did I miss?" I hugged Janie in an apology.

"Let's get out of this neighborhood, and I'll tell you," said Janie. "Which way, Edmund?"

We slunk through the street, one by one, clinging close to the shadows of the buildings. It wasn't until we reached the lighted bridge we had crossed earlier that Janie came to a halt. "There's enough light here."

"For what?"

"To read what Harry wrote on that five pound note, doofus."

Thirty-three

"Mind the gap."

"Why does she keep saying that?"

"Who?"

"That woman saying, 'Mind the gap,' 'Mind the gap.' "

"Honey, that's recorded, and the reminder is to keep you from stepping in the gap between the train and the rails."

"I only need to be told once."

"I heard her enough yesterday to ask her home to marry my brother . . . that is, if I had a brother."

"Minnie, you're sure we're in the right place?"

"Marble Arch station. Two o'clock train."

"It could be the train going the other way. The note didn't say which way."

"Which is why we put Janie and Edmund on that track."

"But I want to be on the right track. I mean the correct track. I want to see Harry."

"And I want you to see him. Believe me, I want you to see him."

"Do people really step through that gap?"

"Yep, just like they step in front of cars and buses when they cross a street. That's why they paint those arrows on the sidewalk so tourists won't get hit because they are used to looking for traffic the other way."

"What time is it?"

"The same one-forty-five it was when you asked me thirty seconds ago."

"Do you see anyone that looks like Harry?"

"No."

"What if the train's not on time? Do you think he'll be on the train or get on with us?"

"I honestly don't know. All the note said was Marble Arch station. Two o'clock train. What do you think it means? You're the one who knows Harry best."

"I don't think I know Harry at all."

It had been a busy morning for us. Our reservations at Selfridges had run out. Three nights was all even an influential Minnie had been able to arrange, and we had to move out by checkout time. It was Janie's idea for us to move to Twenty Wigmore Street. "It's your flat, after all."

"It's not my flat now. Harry's alive. It was just my flat while Harry was dead," I reminded her.

"Well, the sentiment is the same. He'd want you to be there, I know it."

"You want us to be there. Then you could say you had a flat in London."

"Girls, girls, don't squabble. I agree with Janie, Honey. Moving to Harry's flat is a good idea. We can do it ourselves. Just carry the bags across the street and no hassle with trying to find another hotel. And we don't know how much longer we'll have to be here. You know I'm going to have to leave soon. I have that shoot in Wales. And, Honey, you haven't forgotten the Constant deal, have you? When are you supposed to do that?"

"Tomorrow. I'm meeting them at their office, and we're going for cocktails, but I'll break the appointment if I have to. It all depends on what Harry has to say."

We moved.

Minnie seduced the clerk at Wigmore again with camera smiles and folded pound notes while Janie and I hustled the bags up the stairs. I set to cleaning up the mess the vandals had created, and Janie and Minnie headed off to Selfridges's food court. There was only a can of coffee and half a bottle of gin in Harry's cabinets. "I don't think he stayed here very much," noted Janie. "And it's such a lovely flat." She bought daffodils for the kitchen windowsill and waved at the workers across the street at the IBM building.

I even found an adapter in one of Harry's drawers and was finally able to plug in my laptop computer. I had E-mail from Steven Hyatt. I shared it with the others, reading aloud and editing out the part where he said he loved me.

"Steven says they've finished shooting the last scenes, and he's headed back to Hollywood. He just sent this. Looks like he's been out of touch in the outback and only arrived back in Sydney. Anyway, he's on a plane by now. Oh, and he got my message that we're in London, and he hopes we're having a wonderful time."

Minnie rolled her eyes. "Write him back and tell him we're having a ball. Tell him we're working on a new script for him about kidnappers and murders and crazy mothers. Tell him that in the end, the butler does it . . . with the upstairs maid."

"Minnie! I can't write him that." But I did.

Around noon, Edmund joined us for sandwiches from Selfridges's take-away counter and refused to take money for the day's adventure. "Coo, I'm part of this now. You've already paid me enough for two weeks' work, anyway. This day is on the house. I wouldn't miss it for the world."

We were in our places by one-thirty.

"It's two o'clock, and no train," I complained to Minnie.

"When have you ever known a train to run on time?"

"There it is. Oh, here it comes. I'm getting nervous."

From her taller vantage point, Minnie looked around at the crowd. "No Harry. No Masud."

"And no Sledge?"

"Well, if he's as tall as you said, then no. No one is looking me in the eye, anyway."

The long silver train snaked into the station and the automatic doors hissed open. Passengers got off, and those behind us pushed to let us know we were holding up the queue. Minnie took a deep breath and said, "Okay, lets get on this car. Mind the gap."

"I can't believe you said that."

People pushed in close behind us, and I grabbed for a strap as the train took off. I missed the strap and lurched into a man in back of me. "I'm sorry," I said. He grunted a reply and pushed me toward the front of the train. "I said I'm sorry," I repeated as I looked around for Minnie. I saw her behind me, blocked by half a dozen passengers, her eyes wide open with fright. Following her gaze, I looked down to see that the man pushing me was an awful beggar looking fellow; his hair stood out from his bald crown in dirty rolls of tangled knots and he was wearing clothes so filthy that they were colorless.

I stifled a scream as the derelict kept pushing me from behind. I looked vainly for an unoccupied seat, but they were all full, and everyone was ignoring my plight. The two of us wound up behind the Plexiglas partition at the front of the train. Two small empty benches were in front of the glass. I sank down on one of them. "What do you want? Just leave me alone," I said, my anger finally coming to the forefront.

"Will you marry me?"

"I beg your pardon. You have a nerve . . . oh, Harry! It's you."

"At your service, luv."

"You look terrible. It's a good disguise. I just don't know what it is that you're disguised for. Everyone said you were dead. Did you know that your mother thinks you're dead?"

Harry interrupted me. "Keep looking down. Don't look at me. We don't have much time."

Instinctively, I looked around instead of down as instructed. "I don't see anyone. Not anyone suspicious. Not Masud, anyway." I looked at Harry out of the corner of my eye and saw him scratching his dirty head like he didn't have a care in the world. Chunks of matted dirt fell to the floor between us, and I didn't have to pretend to be disgusted.

Harry sounded angry when he responded, "Yes, I heard what Masud did to you. I'll get them for that, Honey."

"How did you hear about the kidnapping? I don't want anyone getting anyone. I just want us to all be safe and this to be over. When will it be over, Harry? Masud said you killed his brother and that he was going to kill you. Is that why you were living in Padre? You were hiding from Masud?"

"Hush, dear, and listen to what I say. There's a stop coming up, and I want you to get off and take your friend, the pretty one."

"Minnie," I said and then I hushed and listened.

Thirty-four

"I'm going to adopt a king," Janie said as she came down the hall after her shower. She was towel drying her hair, and before either Minnie or I could come up with one smart retort, she added, "He's for my book. I have decided to go ahead and write my own mystery book, and I'm going to use a king." She took the towel off her head and looked at us. "What?"

"Nothing," I said.

"The king as the detective. I like it," said Minnie.

"Oh, okay. Well, I need a good king, but I can't decide which one. I don't know much about kings. I don't even know who came first—or who's old and who's new."

"You go by the numbers, I think," I told her. "Like Charles I came before Charles II."

"I know them. They're the dark ones with the big hair who lost their heads. Everyone knows them. I want an obscure king to be my hero. That's why I need you to help me."

Minnie blew into the air toward her feet as if the gust would hasten the drying polish on her toes. "Oh, I don't know much about kings, Janie."

And I nodded my head in agreement.

"That's okay, all I want you to do is draw one for me."

"I don't do portraits, either," Minnie laughed. "Maybe I could manage a caricature."

"I mean draw from the stack," and Janie thrust a deck of cards toward us. "It's the official Kings and Queens of England deck. I've shuffled them. Now you pick me a king."

"What if I draw a queen?"

"Then we'll put her back in the stack. Go on, Honey. Pick a card."

I complied and handed her Richard III.

"Oh, I know him, and we can't use him. He's been overdone. Here, your turn, Minnie."

"Edward VI."

"It says here on the card that he died when he was fifteen. He won't do."

I leafed through the cards. "Here's one for you.

Henry I. He's one of the few in here that say he was a *just and competent ruler*."

"Yes, I want a good one so he can ferret out the bad. Henry I. Okay, Henry, you're mine." She read Henry's card as she headed toward the bedroom. "Wait, how do I find out about him? For background and all?"

Minnie was putting all her pedicure equipment back in her pink cosmetic bag, one of many she carried around the country, and said, "I'd try the Barbican. It's kind of like a time line museum. You walk through by ages. I learned more about English history there than anywhere else. You can look up the address in my Fodor's."

"Great. Leave it for me when you go? Today is my day to be a tourist in London. Isn't it great to have life back to normal? You, going on an audition with Edmund and Honey meeting with the book people? Harry alive and . . . Oh, maybe not everything is back to normal. But, bottom line, he's alive. You know, Honey, you've been a bit mysterious about when you're seeing him again. In person. Not in disguise. I mean we've come through a hurricane, survived a tornado and one kidnapping. We've even come to a foreign country to find him. All you said last night was that everything was fine. I think we're due an explanation here."

I drank a sip of my coffee and waved my own
toes in the air; Minnie was kind enough to do double pedicures. "Mysterious? Was I? I didn't mean
to be." I guided the conversation. "I've been trying
to think about whether I should say yes to him—
about getting married."

I was embarrassed when my ploy worked.

"Getting married? He asked you again? Oh, let's
do it on this trip. I know the greatest chapel, the
Winchester Registry. I went to a wedding there
once." Minnie was already planning her brides-
maid dress.

Janie cut to the core of the matter. "And just
where does that leave Steven Hyatt? And don't
forget that, although we dearly love Harry, he *is* a
murderer. Don't you want to know the rest of *that*
story?"

Well, yes, I did. And as soon as I could get them
on their way, I *would* know it. Harry had been
specific about my coming alone to meet him. Not
that he didn't like Janie and didn't want to meet
Minnie. "It will be safer with just one of you,"
he'd whispered across the aisle of the shaking
train. "Come alone, please." That's why I didn't
dare tell them all of Harry's conversation. I knew
my friends and knew they wouldn't let me out of
the flat without their protection.

I changed the direction of the conversation

again. "Speaking of Steven Hyatt, I had another E-mail from him. He's just arrived back in the States and wants to know what's going on over here."

"What did you tell him?"

"That we're having a wonderful time and wished he was here. You think for one minute that I'm going to tell him that I was kidnapped and knifed? He'd be here in two shakes of a lamb's tail, and we don't need that." I didn't tell them that Steven, afraid I'd get back together with Harry, had also asked me to marry him in his E-mail. Some women enjoy such a dilemma. It just gave me the cramps.

"And I checked my bank balance on-line. It's still showing zero, so it was a good idea for us to move here. At least we're saving on hotel costs."

The two women got into a discussion of the high cost of everything in England, and that distracted them from their questions about Harry. I wished for the sake of my churning stomach that I could forget them, too.

In the end, I left Wigmore Street first. I just couldn't wait any longer for them to finish getting dressed. I hurriedly found a pink flowered dress that I thought would pass for business attire and ran out the door, telling them I would be late, late, late if I didn't scurry. I went straight to the street phone box and dialed the number for Dragon Flight. I had more trouble knowing how much pence to insert in the slot than I did telling the man who answered that regrettably I would have to postpone our meeting.

Then I hurried to The Breakfast Scene to meet Harry.

It was closed. I hit myself in the head with my palm. "Duh, of course, it's closed. That's why it's called The *Breakfast* Scene." It was going on the two o'clock time I had promised to meet Harry, and the sign on the door said the restaurant closed at one. "Oh, wherever is Harry?"

"Talking to yourself is a sign of dementia," said a voice behind me.

"Harry!" I spun in my tracks to see him.

"Surprise. It's me."

"Sledge!"

"Want to see your Harry? Come with me."

Thirty-five

"Yes, I did kill Masud's brother."

That was Harry's direct answer to my frustrated attempt to make sense of a well-dressed Sledge Hamra taking me by the elbow outside the flat on Wigmore Street and hustling me into a waiting taxi. He'd soothed all my protests and multiple questions with the same canned answer: "Ask Harry."

And ask Harry I did.

The second I saw him. The real Harry. No disguises. Just plain old redheaded Harry, with a laugh ready to spring from his throat. Maybe a bit more formal, no beach cutoffs in this area of London, but the same casual, laid-back style.

Sledge Hamra had paid off the cabby at an in-

tersection near Leicester Square and tugged me
into an alleyway that led to a backstage door of a
theater. "Harry's in here," he'd promised as an en-
ticement for me to enter quietly and not make a
scene on the street.

I followed, hoping that it was a live Harry I
would see.

A very live Harry grabbed me as Sledge and I
entered the building. He glanced at the private investigator to receive the reassuring nod that I took
to mean that we had not been followed, and then
my Harry gave me the most passionate embrace
and kiss he'd ever given me. I responded with genuine emotion to the kisses, it was like a waking
dream to be kissing Harry again. I would have
enjoyed it more had I not known we had a watcher
to our reunion. I opened my eyes to see an amused
Sledge Hamra watching us.

"Who is he?" I asked as I pointed to my escort.

"Sorry. Honey, meet Al Hamra, one of the U.S.
Navy's finest SEALs—and my good friend."

"He tricked me. You tricked me." I declared as
I pulled myself out of Harry's arms.

"Had to—for your own sake. Al's been your
bodyguard for awhile now because . . . well, it's a
long story."

"Pretty poor excuse of a bodyguard if you ask
me," I said. "I've got some questions for you, too,

buddy." And I pointed my mother's accusing finger at the tall man.

Al "Sledge" Hamra shrugged. "Can I help it if
I'm better in the water than on land? I'm not a
bodyguard, just a friend helping out a friend." He
held up his big hands in protest. "Hey, if you're
going to be angry at anyone, please make it
Harry."

So I turned to Harry again who motioned for
me to sit down on an oversized chair in the small
room he'd guided us to. "No one will disturb us
here. It's a script reading room, where the cast and
director do read-throughs on the script when they
begin production or when something's being built
onstage." He sat on one end of a long, blue velvet
couch, and Sledge perched on the arm of the other
end.

"Okay, I'll buy that. 'Cause what I'm hearing
here sounds like a bad script to me." I sounded
harsh because my real self just wanted to grab
Harry and love him till the cows came home, but
I figured this was not the time or the place.

The men looked at each other, and Sledge ges-
tured to Harry to continue his story. "Right. Well,
as I said, luv, I killed Masud's brother . . ."

"Or I did," interrupted Sledge.

An exasperated Harry said, "We've gone over
that, Al. I killed him."

I tried to get comfortable in the big chair but finally had to pull my legs up under me to keep them from dangling on the ground. "Masud thinks Harry did it."

"He thinks Harry did it because that's the only name he had to go on," said Sledge.

"It's like this," said Harry. "It was during the Gulf War. Al and I were collaborating on some Iraq recon missions, and we were doing one in Basra—with another guy from my squad—when we were discovered. And this other man, Robin was his name, and I were captured."

"What happened to you?" I asked Sledge.

"I was across the street, had gone there to make some calculations . . ."

"Calculations?"

"That was our assignment. To get the coordinates of a building known to house military personnel and equipment. Laser coordinates for a bombing mission. We tried to be so careful so we wouldn't get any civilian homes or businesses."

"You just marched in and measured things?"

Harry finally let loose with the laugh he'd been hiding. My heart warmed at the sound of it, but I was still more angry and curious than forgiving. "No, no, lass. We were in disguise. You wouldn't have known me. My skin was as dark as Masud's, my hair was black, and I wore black contact lenses. We'd swum in during the night from our ship in the Gulf."

"You swam in? How far out was your ship?"

"About twenty-five miles, and no, we didn't swim all the way. A helicopter flew us nearer the beach—we'd taken out most of their radar by that time in the war—*then* we swam in."

"It's not like we hadn't done it before," said Sledge. "We were the best at doing recon."

"Then what went wrong?"

"What usually goes wrong? Someone was where they weren't supposed to be, according to our information. And a crew showed up to take us. It was just Robin and me, as I said, Al was out of it, across the street."

"I saw it all, though. They fired at Robin and Harry. Hit them both." Sledge paused and added casually, "So, I just went in and got them, or Harry, anyway. Couldn't rescue Robin." He had a regretful grimace on his face as he talked. "Turned out these were a group of terrorist trainees, not military. Masud's brother was shot and killed. Military might have chalked it up to war games, but Masud took it as a personal vendetta."

I was awestruck at the courage of these men. Quietly, I asked, "And how did they get your name, Harry? How did Masud know it was you?"

"Robin," he answered just as quietly. "And trust

me, he didn't give up my name lightly. We heard
later when we found out Masud had targeted me."

"He's dead?"

"Yes. We went back in quickly with reinforce-
ments, but he was dead. Well, Al went back in, I
was in hospital."

"How did you know Masud was after you?"

Al answered, "There was an attempt on Harry's
life while he was in the hospital. We caught the
man, and he finally talked." He sounded bitter as
he went on. "We know how to make prisoners
talk, too, but this guy is still alive."

"How come Masud wasn't after Sledge?" I
couldn't call him Al.

"Robin was new on the squad. I don't think he
even knew my name," answered Sledge.

"That's when you came to Padre?" I asked
Harry.

"Not right away, no. I wandered around some.
Did a lot of recuperating and therapy. You think I
limp now, you should have seen me then. But, yes,
I finally wound up in Padre. I just couldn't do the
Mexican thing, but I got as close to the border as
I could. Really thought I was safe. They didn't
have a description of me, just a name."

"So, why didn't you change your name?"

"Stubborn I guess—some pride. And I thought
I was invincible. Actually, I wasn't too worried;

from what I could gather—and the home office did keep me informed—Masud was busy blowing up things all over and teaching terrorism out in the desert. He couldn't keep tabs on me, but we knew who *he* was, and the government kept a close watch on him."

"So you were safe until you came back to England?"

"Right. My mother really was ill. Well, you saw her; I don't have to tell you."

"She looked good, actually, until I mentioned your name."

"Isn't she great? She was an actress here on the stage before she married my father. That's how we get to sit here and be undisturbed. She's still a patron of the theater."

Sledge slid over the arm of the couch and stretched his long legs in front of him as he situated himself on the couch. "Turns out, someone's been keeping a watch out for Harry for Masud. Although he was discreet when he returned, this spy told Masud that Harry was back. They'd been keeping a watch on his mother's house, you see. But they also followed him to Wigmore Street."

I nodded slowly. "I'm beginning to understand now. To keep Masud away, you faked your death?"

"Yes, and I couldn't get in touch with Al—he's

living in Saint Louis now, by the way—and he sent you the key."

"Her Majesty's government informs me you're dead, I did like you said, sent the key to the dog at Honey's. Put that sucker in the mail two hours before Harry calls to say he's okay."

"And you came to Fort Worth . . . and I found you at Bondesky's looking for . . . what?"

"The key to Wigmore Street. Harry said this Bondesky had it, and first I should get it from him. How did I know the guy would go bonkers and take a powder? Anyway, you found the key first, so I just stuck around and kept an eye on you like Harry said to do."

"And that's why Bailey liked you so much? He knew you from when you visited Harry? And you'd already taught him that trick, hadn't you? But, why did you mail the key to him and not to me?"

"My idea," answered Harry. "It was meant to be a last joke between us, Honey, something to make you smile when you remembered me. Steven Bondesky had all the hard answers, the legal ones, but with him gone, the joke backfired, and you became more involved than I ever wanted you to be. Also, it was meant to throw Masud off track. I didn't know then if he knew about you or not." He got up and came to sit on the arm of my chair, his fingers lightly brushing the thin red scars on my face. He said angrily, "Turns out he did know about you, didn't he? Honey, I'm so sorry you got caught up in this."

I didn't like the look in Harry's eyes, so I turned to Sledge as I put two and two together. "And the note on Bailey's dog food bowl?"

Sledge raised his hand. "Me. Didn't know the damned thing ripped. I went in Harry's in the dark. Thought I got it all. Figured if you didn't find anything, you'd just head back to Fort Worth."

"And you did kill that man in the hurricane?"

"Didn't mean to. Meant to just disarm him. I was waiting around outside to make sure you and Janie were safe, when I saw him approach the bookstore. There *was* a hurricane going on, if you remember. I recognized him as one of Masud's stateside recruits. Guess I hit him harder than I thought. I think he drowned though, I don't think he died from me hitting him. Not directly. And, Honey, I'm sorry about the kidnapping, too. We didn't know that Masud was watching the airport for you. They got your picture from Harry's apartment. I'm not a very good bodyguard, am I? Actually, I'm a lawyer in Saint Louis."

"Sledge?"

"Yes?"

"Where's my microwave?"

Thirty-six

I'd returned to Wigmore Street about six to find Janie ecstatic about Henry I and Minnie trying on a new outfit from Liberty's.

"Henry is so exciting, Honey. He died from overeating. He reminds me of Twyman Towerie in that respect. Think what fun I'll have with that in the book. Oh, and his daughter Matilda, now that's a character for you."

"They had this fab sale at Liberty's, Honey, we've all got to go tomorrow. Oh, and I'm going to the theater with Edmund tonight. He got comp tickets to *The Phantom*. Bless his heart, I didn't have it in me to tell him I've seen it twenty times in three countries. Have ya'll seen it? We'll go tomorrow night after we shop."

"We're running a little low on cash to be shopping, not to mention what a play would cost," I reminded Minnie.

"Pooh, I've got millions, and it will be my treat. One head-to-toe outfit for both of you. And I get to choose them. Don't give me that look, Honey Huckleberry. If it makes you feel better, you can pay me back when you find your money again, and did I mention that I won't be coming home tonight?"

"Oh, no."

"What? Silly, it's just Edmund. He's so down over not getting a part in the new play today, I thought . . . well . . . I thought I'd just cheer him up."

"That part is fine; it's the not being home that worries me. I have to go out, too. I'm having dinner with the Dragon Flight representatives." It gagged me to lie to them again. "That will leave Janie here alone."

Janie mimicked Minnie. "Pooh, I'll be just fine. I have Henry the Very First to keep me company. I'm tired, anyway. I'll just take a bath and snuggle in and maybe get into the mood for writing by emulating Henry. There's pimento cheese and chocolate cake and tons of fresh fruit here. I'll just take a crash course in overeating." She headed back toward the bathroom. "Honey, you never did tell us for sure when you're meeting with Harry."

I gagged again. "Tomorrow. Tomorrow for sure."

"Well, I hope so," she called out from the bathroom. "There's still a lot I don't understand."

Minnie pulled a black stocking up her mile-high leg, "Me, either. And that Masud? Harry thinks he's no problem anymore? That's what you said." She was wearing gold Capri pants and a scarlet silk top. I hoped I lived through the night to go shopping with her tomorrow. Anything Minnie picked out was sure to beat those Peter Pan collared things my mother always chose.

Before I had to gag again, there was a knock on the door. Minnie arched her eyebrows at me, but I wouldn't open the door until I found out who it was. "It's only Edmund, silly," she said.

They left for dinner and the theater while I sat down at the dining table and opened my laptop. The problem was, I didn't know who to tell my story to.

Finally I E-mailed Evelyn Potter.

Dear Evelyn, I hope you and Kantor are enjoying the house. Yes, I agree it's a strange place to live, but I wish I were there right now. We're having an interesting time here. Janie has decided to write a novel, and tell

Kantor he better hurry with his book, or Janie will knock him off the best-seller list. Ha ha. She is thoroughly engrossed in research for the book. Minnie, whom you've never met, is dating Edmund, whom you've never met. He's our driver and an actor. Although the latter description is still to be proven.

That's all the news here.

Well, there is this one thing.

I told you we had found Harry alive and well. That's not exactly true. He's alive all right, but still pursued by the men who kidnapped me. I did tell you about the kidnapping, didn't I? The scars are healing and makeup covers my eye, which has turned yellow. Anyway, I'm sure this is boring to you, but I wanted someone to know what's going on.

I'm going out tonight to lure Masud (the kidnapper) to Harry. Now, before you go getting excited, it was my idea, not Harry's. I had a hard time convincing him that I could be bait to catch Masud. I had help from Sledge Hamra. Did I tell you that he has turned out to be a good guy? And, oh, yes, you will find the key to a storage locker over on Magnolia Avenue under the red Fosteria lamp on the side table in the living room. All my stuff is there, the microwave, TV, etc. Sledge took them as a poor excuse to make us think he was really broke and crooked. He and Harry thought if I knew who Sledge really was, I'd come looking for Harry. Which, of course, is what I did anyway. I'd appreciate it if Kantor could collect the stolen goods that weren't stolen after all. I'll pay him back when I come home. That is, if I have money. Have you heard from Bondesky?

Guess that's it then.

If we don't stop Masud tonight, he will eventually kill Harry. No one should have to live like that, do you think?

One more thing: If anything happens to me, which it won't, of course, please note that I want everything I have to go to Janie. The money, too, if Bondesky can find it. Give my love to Steven Hyatt, but please don't tell him a word of this. And hug Bailey for me.

Hope I haven't worried you.
Love, Honey Huckleberry

p.s. Didn't mean to be so formal. I said Honey Huckleberry so that if you need to show this to some lawyer, it will be legal. Bye for good now.

Janie came back into the living room, a glass of milk and a slice of cake in her hand. She was wearing a large, white cotton gown and her face was shiny from her Ponds cream. "Oops, I thought you were gone. You caught me. Yes, I'm eating my dessert first. It won't matter in the long run, now will it?"

I looked at her fondly. It might well be the last time I saw her. My eyes misted with tears.

"Okay, then. If it means so much to you, I'll fix a sandwich first. Geesh."

I stopped her as she turned toward the kitchen. "No, no, sweetie, you eat your cake. I was just thinking how much I love you. How much you've come to mean in my life. I'm glad you came to live with me, Janie."

"Are you sure? I can do pimento first. And I love you, too, Honey. Honey, is something wrong? Are you all right?"

I was saved from another lie by the phone in the hall. I answered on the second ring to hear Minnie's hysterical voice. "Honey, thank God. I swear I saw those Masud goons outside the building. I just knew they had you again. I want you to bar the door with something, maybe the dining table, and call the police."

"Where are you?" I asked.

"At the theater. Edmund and I came on here,

but we can come back. The more I thought about those men outside Wigmore Street, the more worried I became."

"Minnie, I assure you, Harry told me on the tube that Masud wasn't a danger anymore. He . . . he . . . he's being watched. And there are lots of Arabs in London, haven't you noticed? I'm sure you didn't see Masud. And everything is just fine here. Go, enjoy your play." Well, shoot, if I didn't have to tell a lie in the living room, I had to tell one in the hall.

Minnie hung up only after I reassured her for the tenth time that I would cancel my dinner with the book reps and stay right in the flat with Janie.

"Who was that on the phone?" Janie wanted to know.

"The representative from Dragon Flight, confirming our plans for tonight," I told her. I was getting so good at lying my stomach didn't even flip-flop.

I picked up my purse and started out the door.

"Aren't you going to change your clothes? You wore that dress this afternoon when you met with them. And you're really not going to wear that hat, are you? And you at least should put some more makeup on that eye."

"Bye, Janie," I said and left.

• • •

"Did you know that I looked it up on-line and that your name, Masud, means *happy* in your language?" I asked the man who took me by the elbow and ushered me to a curbside car. "I bet your mother wouldn't be very *happy* to know what you've done with your life."

Masud shoved me into the backseat and looked around for witnesses. "I never knew my mother," he said as he joined me in the backseat.

"Why does that not surprise me?" I muttered under my breath as the car eased into the London traffic.

Thirty-seven

Oh, how Harry had argued, vehemently and violently that in no way, shape, or fashion was I to be involved in catching Masud.

"Well, you *could* go stand on a street corner and say, 'Hey, Massie, I'm over here. Come and get me.' But then that might involve a lot of innocent bystanders, 'cause sure as shootin', he'd be coming with guns loaded," said Sledge. "And not only that, you've already tried to lure him out in the open when you hired on as bartender at the Royal Raven."

"Couldn't the military help?" I asked.

"They are, Honey, but this man has more hidey holes than your B'rer Rabbit. I hear what you're saying, Al. If I show myself to them, they'll just shoot me and whoever is in the way. That's what would have happened if they had recognized me at the Raven; I know that now. I was just so desperate to get them away from Honey."

We'd sat in the theater for another hour or so making plans and discarding them. Finally, Harry gave in to the one Sledge and I thought was the best. "It's against all my inclinations that I agree. I want you two to know that. I would never, ever use a woman to set a trap."

"She's going to be just fine, Harry. It's you Masud wants. And I'll be there, and we'll be forewarned and armed. You've just got to remember to duck, Honey."

We spent some more time getting me to memorize the directions to Harry's country home. Given my sense of directions, that was no easy task, but eventually I could cite the correct route to the house.

Of course, I forgot it by the time I was seated by Masud himself. I was so caught up in the pretense of acting that I was reluctant to give them the information, that I honestly couldn't remember if it was M2 or M20 that led the way to Harry. All I could scream—when the man in the front seat drew the knife I remembered so well was, "The country. He's in the country. At his mother's house in the country." I was very relieved that they knew where the house was; the front-seat goon pocketed the knife, and Masud sat back, grinning. I must have given a convincing performance. They stopped at a phone box and made some calls and after some nods, got back in the car and we were on our way to what I hoped was the final adventure.

I regretfully watched as the lights of London receded; here I was a tourist and hadn't even gotten to enjoy the sights. "*O rare,* Honey Huckleberry," I whispered as we sped southward.

Exhausted by the day's events, I fell into a semisleep in which I kept reciting, "Walks like a duck, talks like a duck, must be a duck. Duck. Duck." I was horrified on returning to reality to find that I had fallen over on the shoulder of Masud, who was sound asleep, snoring loudly, no doubt dreaming of his own ducks.

"That's Harry's house?" I asked with some surprise. Lord, it was a castle. No, I corrected myself; it was a gorgeous Georgian house with lots of rooms. Lots and lots of rooms. Harry had told me that his grandfather had bought the house in the late '30s and although it dated back for ages and ages, the *real* castle was just over the hill.

"This is where we find Harry Armstead, yes?"

"No. Oh, wait; don't go getting excited on me. He's here, but not in the house. He's been hiding out in the old ruins. You can't drive there. You have to walk through the gardens behind the house. The ruins are just over that hill. They're kinda on a bluff." I spoke as if I knew what I was talking about, but I had never set eyes on this place before. As long as Masud believed me, it didn't matter.

"I can wait here," I told him, trying one of the safety ploys Harry had urged, but Masud grabbed me by the shoulder and pulled me out of the car. "Or I can go with you."

We crossed over the lawn and through the back gardens. Ordinarily, I would have been agog at the sight. Even under these circumstances, I couldn't resist saying, "Would you look at this? It's a white garden. That means that everything that blooms here is a white flower. It's made for moonlit nights like this, don't you think?" My mouth was going faster than my legs, which was a sure indication to me that I was scared stiff.

But even the terrorists were struck dumb by the sight of the castle silhouetted against the moonlit sky. We scrambled across the low stone wall and stood and looked at the building, which had defied time and seemed to me to exist only for tonight and tonight's affair. It loomed three stories tall, and the moon shone through the tall, arched windows, making it seem alive and waiting.

Masud pushed me forward, toward the castle

keep. I stumbled over a loose stone and, as I caught myself on the terrorist's arm, I looked back at the main house. A car was coming up the drive. *The military,* I thought. *Harry did call for backup. Hope Masud doesn't see it.* I recovered from my stumble and ran toward the castle. The three men followed, never looking back.

There was a long, low building next to the tower, but it was dark and uninviting. Instinctively, we entered the high archway of the keep, where suddenly the moon failed us. The man who was the driver turned on his flashlight. It only gave a weak glow in the dark entrance, but he motioned for me to go first up the stone steps that led up the tower. Then he held his finger to his lips, a reminder for me to be silent in my ascent.

I tried, but I stumbled and made more noise than my escorts liked. One shook me by the shoulder, warning me. *Oh, yeah,* I thought. *Like you three don't sound like elephants. It's not easy climbing castle steps in silence.*

When we reached the first landing, Masud held me back, and one of the men explored the two rooms that opened out onto the stairs. He returned, shaking his head, and so we continued upward.

The second landing was larger than the first, and fallen boulders from the peak of the tower littered the area. The hole created by the fallen stones let in the moonlight. We could see clearly that there was only one door at the top of the keep. The door slowly opened, and all our eyes turned to it. The man with the knife started toward it, but Sledge Hamra scared us all by jumping from his dark hiding place behind the toppled stones. Sledge lunged for the terrorist leader, but the man with the knife was between them. Masud jerked me tightly against him. From below, I could hear the sounds of others running up the stairs. *Please hurry,* I gave a silent prayer to the rescuers below. *This isn't going well.* The knife bearer intercepted Sledge, and they struggled on the floor. A gun went off.

"Duck, Honey." Harry's voice came out of the dark.

I fell to the floor next to Sledge and his assailant. Both were too quiet on the stone floor. I looked up to see Harry come out of the tower room with his gun pointed at Masud. "Give it up, Masud," he yelled.

With me out of reach, Masud grabbed the driver with one hand and thrust him into the line of fire. With his other hand, he aimed his gun at Harry. They both fired at the same time. The driver and Harry fell with a thud.

I hunched over Sledge's body, and Masud aimed his gun at me. "You tried to set me up. Now you are dead, too." He kept the weapon aimed at me but turned his sloe eyes to cover the stairs where the noise was increasing.

I groped around for a rock or something, anything, to throw at Masud. Instead, I found Sledge's gun in his hand. It was easy to pry it from his fingers; they lay loose and limp around the handle. I aimed the gun at Masud, who had become distracted with the arrival of who I had thought was to be our rescuers.

To my surprise, I heard Masud say smugly, "Ah, good. You found the house. You are too late though. Harry Armstead is dead. I have triumphed. We don't need her."

I thought he meant he didn't need *me*, but when I looked to see who had arrived, I was horrified to see Janie in her long, white, flowing gown and shiny Ponds face staring down at me. One of the strangers had his hand over her mouth. Her eyes were wide with fear and astonishment.

I aimed Sledge's gun at Masud. "Let her go," I demanded. I didn't know how to fire a gun, but Masud's white shirt made a good target in the moonlight. How hard could it be?

Masud thwarted my plan by pulling Janie in front of him, and he hid behind her as he had earlier hid behind his dead accomplice and me. She was too scared to speak. Was she too scared to think?

"Janie," I said calmly. "Are you a dead dog?"

Janie went down in a heap, a white cloud of gown at an astonished Musad's feet. He tried to grab her, but her Pond's-slicked neck just slipped out of his grasp.

He shot me anyway.

I had never been shot before. I had never shot a gun before. Both of those deficiencies in my life were erased in the blink of an eye.

I shot and killed Masud before the pain of the bullet in my right leg registered, but when it did, a red-hot haze filled me. It was through this blinding fog that I saw Masud's body fall toward one of the men who had brought Janie into the tower. The dead Masud acted like a lead domino; his catapulting body pushed the man down the stairs, crushing him with his weight. I heard him cry out and then there was silence.

The second man looked at me with my gun still bravely held high. He raised his hands and backed away, backed down the steps, and I heard him running into the night. He didn't know I was shaken to the bone by the recoil of the gun I had fired and paralyzed by the pain in my leg. I couldn't have fired again if the queen herself had demanded it.

I heard Janie scream, and under me, I felt Sledge Hamra stir.

The red haze faded to black.

Thirty-eight

Next year I am going to be thirty.

I've always thought that when I reach thirty, I will Know It All. Somehow—in my mind—that meant that I would wake up on my thirtieth birthday and be wise and solemn, and life would hold no surprises for me. I didn't realize that wisdom comes in increments, meted out by the jeopardys of everyday life. I had lived in a cocoon for so long—one of my own making, to be sure—that I had rushed through the pitfalls of living during the past year. Trying to fulfill my own prophecy of matured utopia, I had fallen over dead bodies, toyed with lovers, spurned authority, and disrupted lives.

And I had killed a man.

No one mentioned the dead terrorist as they gathered around my bedside at the hospital.

That Harry lived was one of the blessings of my life. Before I could dare to ask about him, he had appeared over my bed, his pale face swathed in the gauze bandage that covered the bullet crease near his temple. "Can you ever forgive me?" he asked. Then for the fourth time, "Will you marry me?"

That's what Steven Hyatt asked me, too.

Steven appeared right after I came out of surgery. Masud's bullet had damaged a bone in my thigh, but it hadn't shattered, and there was not going to be permanent damage, I was told.

Steven's thin face hung over my bed. I struggled with a drug-induced cotton mouth to get the words out. "Marry you? Where did you come from?"

"You think Evelyn wouldn't call me after that E-mail of yours? I've been flying all night."

"Where's Janie? Where's Sledge?" I was beginning to come out of the anesthetic, but I was still in a drug-induced world.

"I'm here, Honey. You saved my life." And Janie's face replaced Steven's.

"Too many people in here," said an authoritative voice.

"Yes, Sister, we're leaving," I heard Harry say.

And Janie called out over her shoulder as she

left, "Sledge is out of surgery and is doing well. I was right about him from the first, wasn't I?"

And I was left alone with my tears.

My mother was wrong. That's another thing about finally growing up. You get to say, "My mother was wrong."

"Save your tears," she had instructed. *"People die every day. You can't cry for them all. Save your tears for someone you care about."*

I hadn't cared about Masud, but I cried for him.

Epilogue

"Telephone call for you, miss." The attending sister handed me the receiver.

"Huckleberry, what? I can't go off and leave you for a day or two without you getting in tall grass?"

"Bondesky?"

"In the flesh, Huckleberry. Heard you was worried about me. So I came on home. You been up to shenanigans while I was gone, I hear. What? You can't get in enough trouble here in Texas?"

"It's wonderful talking to you, too, you old reprobate. You're back in Fort Worth?"

"Yeah, where you should be. When you coming home?"

A different kind of haze enfolded me. A warm, white one that signaled security and love. This old man had loved me most of my life. He'd unobtrusively been my lifeline while I'd searched for my own. Maybe mother *was* right; more tears came to my eyes. I hurried to fill him in. "I'll be able to travel soon, they say. Janie's here with me. She's writing a book, a murder of her own. I'm at the sanitarium where Harry's mother is recovering. Not that she needs to recover now. Harry's fine and safe. Bondesky, he wants me to marry him, and so does Steven Hyatt."

"So who will it be, Huckleberry, the knight or the showman?"

"I'll tell you like I told them—neither. For now. I have to grow up first, but I'll know by my birthday. I'll be grown next year. I'll decide then."

"I'll put money on it, Huckleberry."

"Speaking of money, Bondesky . . ."

EARLENE FOWLER

introduces Benni Harper, curator of San Celina's folk
art museum and amateur sleuth

❏ **FOOL'S PUZZLE**　　　　**0-425-14545-X/$6.50**
Ex-cowgirl Benni Harper moved to San Celina, California, to
begin a new career as curator of the town's folk art museum. But
when one of the museum's first quilt exhibit artists is found dead,
Benni must piece together a pattern of family secrets and small-
town lies to catch the killer.

❏ **IRISH CHAIN**　　　　**0-425-15137-9/$6.50**
When Brady O'Hara and his former girlfriend are murdered at the
San Celina Senior Citizen's Prom, Benni believes it's more than
mere jealousy–and she risks everything to unveil the conspiracy
O'Hara had been hiding for fifty years.

❏ **KANSAS TROUBLES**　　　　**0-425-15696-6/$6.50**
After their wedding, Benni and Gabe visit his hometown near
Wichita. There Benni meets Tyler Brown: aspiring country singer,
gifted quilter, and former Amish wife. But when Tyler is murdered
and the case comes between Gabe and her, Benni learns that her
marriage is much like the Kansas weather: bound to be stormy.

❏ **GOOSE IN THE POND**　　**0-425-16239-7/$6.50**
❏ **DOVE IN THE WINDOW**　**0-425-16894-8/$6.50**

SUSAN WITTIG ALBERT

__THYME OF DEATH   0-425-14098-9/$6.50

China Bayles left her law practice to open an herb shop in
Pecan Springs, Texas. But tensions run high in small towns,
too—and the results can be murder.

__WITCHES' BANE   0-425-14406-2/$5.99

When a series of Halloween pranks turns deadly, China must
investigate to unmask a killer.

__HANGMAN'S ROOT   0-425-14898-X/$5.99

When a prominent animal researcher is murdered, China
discovers a fervent animal rights activist isn't the only person
who wanted him dead.

__ROSEMARY REMEMBERED   0-425-15405-X/$5.99

When a woman who looks just like China is found murdered
in a pickup truck, China looks for a killer close to home.

__RUEFUL DEATH   0-425-15941-8/$5.99
__LOVE LIES BLEEDING   0-425-16611-2/$5.99
__CHILE DEATH   0-425-17147-7/$6.50